SECRET SANTA

SECRET SANTA

RICHARD GRANT BENNETT

BRYCE CLARK

JASON deVILLIERS

SWEETWATER
BOOKS
an imprint of Cedar Fort, Inc.
Springville, Utah

ISBN 13: 978-1-4621-1739-0

Published by Sweetwater Books, an imprint of Cedar Fort, Inc.
2373 W. 700 S., Springville, UT, 84663
Distributed by Cedar Fort, Inc., www.cedarfort.com

LIBRARY OF CONGRESS CATALOGING-IN-PUBLICATION DATA

Bennett, Richard Grant, 1978- author.
Secret Santa / Richard Grant Bennett, Bryce Clark, Jason deVilliers.
     pages cm
Summary: "Agent Noel Green only has horrible memories from his past Christmases. He becomes the head of Santa's Secret Service in order to protect Santa and keep the joy in other children's Christmases. He hires Veronica Snow as Santa's new PR rep who faces the difficult task of keeping the image of Santa strong without giving away his secrets. Santa's terminated elf, Cole, has sworn to get rid of Santa and destroy the Naughty List. He notices Green's affection for Snow and kidnaps her as the weak spot of the secret service. The SSS manages to rescue Snow and destroy Cole's lair. Cole's last attempt of getting to Santa is at his appearance at the Macy's Thanksgiving Day parade. His attack leads to a flying sleigh chase over the Manhattan skyline. The SSS manages to capture Cole over the Rockefeller Plaza and save Christmas."--Description from publisher.
ISBN 978-1-4621-1739-0 (hardback : alk. paper)
1. Santa Claus--Fiction. 2. Christmas stories. I. Clark, Bryce, author. II. DeVilliers, Jason, 1975- author. III. Title.
PS3602.E4695S43 2015
813'.6--dc23
                         2015011169
Cover illustration by Susan Keller
Cover design by Michelle May
Cover design © 2015 by Lyle Mortimer
Edited and typeset by Justin Greer

Printed in the United States of America
10 9 8 7 6 5 4 3 2 1
Printed on acid-free paper

For our fathers:
Thanks for keeping the lights on . . .

PART ONE

CHAPTER ONE

High above the earth, inside a cumulous cloud formation, the cold of night caused the temperature to shift to 14 degrees Fahrenheit. At that exact moment, a particle of dust entered the cloud and collided with a water droplet as it was freezing. This reaction created an ice crystal that was circular in shape. Instantly, other water droplets and water vapor froze onto the crystal, creating six distinct arms extending out from its center.

As this new formation gained mass, it fell toward the earth below, passing twinkling stars aligned in storied patterns across the sky and the moon, full and bright.

This formation, as it was created inside the cloud, would be known as snow when it hit the ground, which it did, just seconds later, joining millions of others like it, though each slightly different.

The snowflake had landed in the middle of Lincoln Avenue, an all-American neighborhood decorated in preparation for the holiday to come the following day.

Vivid blinking lights dotted houses and trees. Inflatable reindeer and snowmen were perched on snow-covered lawns. Inside many of the homes, milk and cookies had been laid out near ornately adorned trees, and stockings had been hung with what could legitimately be called care.

And one thing that stood out, house to house, was how still things were both inside and out. A distinct quiet hung over the entire town, the kind of quiet that could only be pierced by something special, something grand.

* * *

Above Lincoln Avenue, two black stealth F-22 fighter jets blasted through the night sky. Inside the cockpit, the pilot spoke to his mission control, "Sugarplum Fairy to Nutcracker. Do you copy? Over."

A female voice came back over the radio, "We read you, Sugarplum Fairy. Over."

"We are in position above Lincoln Avenue. Over."

"Roger that, Sugarplum. Everything looks good from here. You have an all clear on Lincoln Avenue. The Beard will close the breach in T-minus 10 seconds. Over."

"Copy that. Making our descent now to provide cover. Over and out."

The pilot clicked off the radio and the fighter jet banked hard to the right and began to drop down closer to the tops of the homes below, but still high enough to maintain the still silence of the slumbering city.

Far below the jet, a dull sucking noise sounded as the air shifted, expanding like an inflating balloon. A flying object shot out of the expanding air, slowing as it sailed toward the rooftops below.

The object was an enormous sleigh, the carriage a custom-made, oversized, red convertible Rolls Royce Phantom with solid gold runners in place of wheels. Inside were three rows of plush leather seats and an expansive dash displaying advanced GPS and communications technology. The rear of the sleigh expanded into an aerodynamic chamber created with the same titanium alloy used on the space shuttle, maximizing the sleigh's velocity and gift hauling capacity.

Nine reindeer pulled the sleigh as they sprinted through the sky. The lead reindeer's glowing red nose provided illumination in the fog. An old man in a red suit guided the vessel from the front seat of the cabin. Even with the latest technology, this old man preferred to use reins, as they were a direct tie between him and the reindeer.

The old man's name was one familiar to people all across the world. It was a name that caused many children to lose several anxious hours of sleep, filled with excitement and joy. It was a name sung about over and over by children in almost every town in nearly every country. It was a name for the ages . . . *Santa Claus.*

Santa called on his reindeer, "On Comet, on Cupid, on Donner, and Blitzen . . ." The sleigh glided toward the array of brightly lit and welcoming rooftops.

While Santa prepared to deliver gifts on Lincoln Avenue, the Command Center at the North Pole was a hive of activity. The operations at the Pole had all the latest technology and were overseen by a very secretive and select organization. This was an organization whose mission had never been revealed or discussed in public because its very nature ran contrary to everything that Santa Claus and Christmas stood for. But even Santa Claus had to face the realities of the world today.

One such reality was that throughout time, influential and powerful figures have faced a stark truth: there are always those who would seek to remove them from power. From Caesar's Praetorian and Britain's Grenadier Guards to the United States' Secret Service, elite groups of highly trained protectors have united with one common purpose: to protect the boss from any and all attacks.

None of the world's leaders have been immune to these threats. Not even the top man at the North Pole. Even Santa Claus needed his own bodyguards, his own private security—his own *Santa's Secret Service.*

And so it was that in the North Pole Command Center, the men and women who worked for Santa's Secret Service manned sophisticated equipment, monitoring Santa's every move and preparing neighborhoods for his secure arrival.

Special Agent Madison Burke wore a headset and sat in front of multiple screens monitoring the activity at Lincoln Avenue. Agent Burke was relatively new to her job at Santa's Secret Service, and it had been a long night. Hundreds of other agents sat at similar stations in the expansive Command Center, monitoring activity all over the world. The stations were aligned on dozens of semi-circular rows facing an enormous screen front and center. Christmas Eve had been highly successful so far, and there were only a few deliveries left.

The agents turned as Head Agent Noel Green confidently entered the room. Green was a handsome man in his late thirties, dressed in a black suit and tie. An official SSS identification badge hung from his right pocket, and a small candy cane pin was perfectly positioned on his left lapel.

Green made his way toward Burke. "Agent Burke!"

"Yes sir," said Burke.

"What is Mr. Claus's twenty?"

"He is making his descent toward Lincoln Avenue in Evanston, Illinois, sir."

Green peered closely at Burke's monitors. "Agent Burke, did you issue a landing clearance for Mr. Claus at this location?"

"Yes sir, I did. Imagery from CLAUS-SAT as well as intelligence from ground crews show secure landing conditions. The coast is clear, sir."

Green pulled over another chair and sat in front of Burke's workspace, pressing buttons, pulling up alternate screens with more data. "I think there might be a problem with your assessment, Agent Burke. Did you reference this neighborhood's history?"

Burke looked down, flustered, knowing immediately that she'd made a major mistake. "Uh . . . no. No, sir. I did not. I thought that—"

Green stood up, interrupting her, as he addressed the entire command center. "C'mon, people! This is day one training stuff here. Always make sure you check the street history before you issue a ground clearance!"

Green turned back to Burke's monitors and pressed a few more buttons. "I'm taking your screen to the main monitor, Agent Burke."

"Yes, sir," said Burke, still kicking herself for her error.

A gigantic screen in the middle of the room lit up with the work Burke had been doing on Lincoln Avenue. The screen began cycling through a massive amount of data concerning that street's history.

Green stood up and put himself directly in front of the screen. Something caught his eye and he lowered his head. "I thought I recognized this street. Listen up, everybody; we have two Class 3 Naughties in play, the McKenzie twins. I'm sure we all remember this redheaded duo of delinquency."

Moans and gripes filled the room as the agents realized what they were dealing with. Burke couldn't take her eyes off her shoes.

"These twerps have topped the naughty list four years in a row. Last year they successfully filmed Mr. Claus landing, and it took our lawyers months to get the footage removed from YouTube!" huffed Green.

Green moved back to Burke's station. He took her headset and put it on. "Come in, Sugarplum Fairy. Do you read?"

Back in the sky over Lincoln Avenue, one of the F-22s pulled up alongside Santa's sleigh. Santa steadied his team, pulling back on the reins. The jet was a safe distance away but it still disturbed the reindeer. They weren't used to sharing the sky that closely.

"Whoa there! Easy!" Santa looked in the direction of the jet and threw his arms up in confusion. The pilot's voice came over a small speaker in the sleigh.

"Sorry, sir. We just received orders from the Pole to divert you to Briar Street due to a Code 9 involving two Naughties. We need to secure the area first, sir," reported the pilot.

"The McKenzie twins," Santa muttered to himself. "Oh, fiddlesticks."

Santa gave the pilot thumbs up, kept the reindeer hovering for a moment, and then altered course.

* * *

Down below on Lincoln Avenue, two unmarked black Chevy Suburbans with flashing red and green lights came speeding down the street, skidding to an ominous stop near a house at the end.

Inside the Chevy, a ground agent in the passenger seat pressed buttons on a sophisticated computer screen mounted within the dash. The screen instantly displayed a thermostatic view of the McKenzie home.

The ground agent sang to himself while he scanned the screen. "We know if you are sleeping, we know if you're . . ." Two human silhouettes appeared on the screen, bright red. ". . . awake!"

The agent at the wheel picked up the radio. "North Pole, we've got a fix on the boys. They're up and appear to be hiding. Over."

Green's voice came back over the radio. "You know what to do, boys. Over."

Inside the McKenzie home, the living room was quiet and serene. An immaculately dressed Christmas tree stood in the corner. Stockings hung and milk and cookies sat on the coffee table, accompanied by a note for Santa.

Two mischievous, eleven-year-old, redheaded twins, Max and Henry McKenzie, hid in the closet and stared at a MacBook with a feed from a webcam they had hidden inside the branches of their Christmas tree.

Now, Henry and Max weren't bad boys on the order of hardened criminals. However, their standard operating procedure was to do the exact opposite of whatever the adults were commanding. And so on Christmas Eve, they had no intention of sleeping. If they could disrupt the traditional order of events, well then, it would truly be a magical holiday for them.

Max whispered to his brother, "Stop pushing buttons, doofus. You're going to mess it up."

"Like you even know what you're talking about, ignoramus. This whole thing was my idea in the first place," said Henry.

* * *

Outside, ground agents wearing night vision goggles quickly made their way toward the house. At the door, the lead agent stopped and pointed upwards. Three other agents pulled out their grappling guns and fired at the roof.

They climbed up the ropes. Once on the roof, the lead agent made his way toward the chimney.

In the closet, the McKenzie boys sat in silence, staring upward.

Max could hardly contain his excitement. "You hear that? There's something on the roof. He's here!"

"Okay, let's go live," said Henry. "Start streaming."

Max pressed a few keys on the laptop and a tiny red light on the webcam glowed. "We're going to be famous," said Max.

Without warning, the sound of compressed air being released came from within the chimney. The boys watched on the computer screen as a thick white mist filled the fireplace and turned the red-hot embers into icy cold crystals.

"What was that?" Henry said.

The boys stared at the laptop, squinting to get a better view of what was happening.

On the screen, they saw a tiny snow globe fall from the chimney and roll into the center of the living room. It let off an intense glow of blinding white light. The screen flashed abruptly to static.

"He nuked our camera! Dad's gonna kill us!" exclaimed Henry.

The boys quietly exited the closet. Henry made his way toward the webcam and Max walked toward the snow globe. The boys didn't see the agents hiding in the shadows.

One agent pulled a tiny silver bell from his belt and threw it into the center of the living room; it jingled as it rolled.

Max spun at the sound. "What the heck?"

"I'm scared," uttered Henry.

Max puffed out his chest and stood as tall as he could, even

9

though his knees were shaking. "Stop being such a baby, Henry!"

The boys crouched over to inspect the curious bell. It let off a high-pitched noise, not unlike a dog whistle, followed by a series of bright red and green flashing lights.

Max and Henry covered their ears. The flashing lights had a hypnotic effect on the boys, and they soon passed out on the living room rug.

The agents emerged from their hiding spots. The lead agent made an 'all clear' signal and spoke into a transmitter on his wrist. "All clear, send in the tech."

A tech agent carried a sleek silver case into the house. He rushed toward the closet where he pulled a disk from the case and slid it into the laptop.

The screen displayed a series of red and green flashing lights. As soon as the lights stopped, the tech agent removed the disk, flashing thumbs up to the lead agent. "Footage erased, sir," whispered the tech agent.

The lead agent nodded. "Excellent work. We better get a diagnostic on the milk and cookies as well."

"Yes, sir." The tech agent hurried over to the milk and cookies and opened his case. Inside were various sophisticated devices. He chose a contraption that had a small opening on one end.

He broke off a tiny portion of the cookie and fed it into the machine. A blinking red light went off.

"We have tainted goodies, sir. Looks like they added Ex-Lax to this batch," said the tech agent.

The lead agent sighed. "Great. That's just what the big guy needs, a Christmas Eve with explosive diarrhea. Better eighty-six those."

The tech agent pulled out a small black bag and dumped the cookies into it.

"North Pole, this is Chimney Sweep," the lead agent spoke into his radio. "Operation successful. The redheaded Naughties are having visions of sugarplums and the footage has been terminated. Lincoln Avenue is secure. Over."

The lead agent leaned away from his radio as he heard the sounds of the North Pole Command Center erupting in celebration.

Agent Green's voice came back. "Good work, Chimney Sweep. Hurricane McKenzie stabilized! Over."

"Just doing our job, sir. Over and out." The lead agent motioned the others toward the fireplace. One by one they entered the chamber of coals and disappeared up the chimney.

The McKenzie twins remained in a deep sleep in front of the fireplace as if the agents had never been there.

Back at the North Pole, in the Operations Room, Green removed the headset and handed it back to an embarrassed Burke.

"That is why we always check a neighborhood's prior history. We just averted months of clean up work. Christmas Eve is the most important night of the year. Everything we do is in preparation for this night. We can't afford slip-ups like these!"

Green looked over the room, then made his way toward the exit. As soon as he was out of the room everyone let out a collective sigh of relief and an older female agent, Betsy, walked over to Burke. "Head up, Burke. That's happened to the best of us."

Burke shook her head. "I don't know . . . Special Agent Green was really upset with me."

Betsy shook her head. "He's like this every year. Don't take it personally."

Burke smiled, somewhat reassured.

CHAPTER TWO

Green made his way down a long hall extending off from the main control room. He thought about the disaster they had just avoided. There were so many things that had to go just right on Christmas Eve and Green had spent much of the night getting air clearance over Washington, DC, and handling a late replacement for Prancer due to an upset stomach. To have the night almost go horribly wrong just at the end would have been devastating. Agent Burke was a promising young agent and had tested highly in training, so to see her make such a crucial mistake was a cause for concern. The agents had to understand that the threats out there were very real, an understanding that was often clouded because they worked for Santa Claus at the North Pole. He felt very strongly that they couldn't let their guard down—ever. In Green's years at the SSS there had never been a major snafu. Green knew better than anybody that the real magic behind the North Pole and Christmas was hard work.

Agent Collins, a young female agent, approached Green, out of breath and anxious. "There you are, sir. I've been looking for you."

"What is it, Agent Collins?" asked Green.

"Miss Snow, sir. She's been taking the North Pole Aptitude Test since early this afternoon."

"Has she finished the NPAT already?" Green looked at his special SSS-issued watch.

"Yes, sir."

"That's a great time, very impressive. How'd she do overall?"

Agent Collins handed him a red folder. "See for yourself. And her time's even better than it appears, sir. She's been in your office waiting for almost an hour."

"Thank you, Collins." Green turned toward his office. He leafed through the folder as he walked. Collins followed close behind.

"Don't you have somewhere to be, agent?"

Collins immediately veered down another corridor.

Green reached his office. It was sparsely decorated, with filing cabinets in one corner, a printer and fax machine in another, and pens, a stapler, and other office supplies arranged precisely on his desk. A gun rack holding multiple Freeze Ray rifles and handguns was on the opposing wall. The only personal effect was a framed photo of his mother.

Green paused as he saw Veronica Snow, a woman in her early thirties sitting in a chair across from his desk. Her back was to him, displaying locks of golden hair that complemented her stylish pant-suit. She turned her head slightly, and Green stared at her for a few moments, somewhat dazed.

Sensing that someone was there, she turned and saw Green and stood to greet him.

"Miss Snow, I'm sorry to have kept you waiting for so long," said Green, breaking out of his daze.

They shook hands, Green's hand a little sweatier than he would have liked. He couldn't help it; her cobalt blue eyes were stunning. Green quickly pulled his hand out of hers, embarrassed at his less-than-professional response.

"I had a situation that needed my attention," Green said as he rounded his desk. "I'm Agent Noel Green. Please have a seat."

They both sat as Green opened the folder on his desk.

"Exactly what agency do you represent, Mr. Green?" asked Veronica. "I've spoken with a few of your employees today, but I still have no idea who you people are."

Green gave her a tight smile, trying to regain control of his emotions. He wasn't going to let the fact that Veronica was beautiful deter him from doing a thorough review of her.

"I'll cover all of that in due time, Miss Snow." Green flipped through the results of Veronica's testing. "These are some of the more impressive NPAT results I've seen."

"Thank you. Although I'm not really sure what it is I'm testing for."

Green continued to peruse the results. He sat up, surprised. "You got a perfect score on the Comprehensive Candy Quiz!"

"Yes, but what do gumdrops and toy soldiers have to do with my aptitude?"

"Nothing. Well . . . everything. Can I offer you a Peep?" He proudly presented a silver cigar box with green Christmas Tree Peeps inside.

"No thank you, Mr. Green. Can we please get to the point? It's Christmas Eve and I still have gifts to wrap. This has all been a very strange experience. I'm only here because someone I trust said it was the opportunity of a lifetime."

"I understand, and if it could have been done any other way, it would have been. But please know that we must maintain the strictest level of security."

"My father was a high ranking officer in the Air Force, Mr. Green. I've been maintaining strict security since I was a toddler. So . . . where are we? Area 51?" Veronica smiled.

"No. That's in the desert. We're up north, and it's freezing outside," said Green, oblivious to Veronica's attempt at humor.

"I know. It was a joke." Veronica rolled her eyes.

"I see. Well, our security does rival that of a government outpost, but we're not actually affiliated with any government. We're a private operation."

"Oil? Is that why you're stationed so far north?"

"Do you understand just how far north you actually are, Miss Snow?"

"No. Why don't you tell me, Mr. Green?" said Veronica, her smile now completely forced and lacking any sincerity.

"You're as far north as you can get," said Green.

Veronica shook her head, annoyed. "Great. So if you're not government and you're not oil, then what exactly are you?"

"Let me start by saying that I've never seen such an impressive résumé. You've handled PR for a who's who list of big-ticket celebrities and high profile politicians. It would appear that you're one of the best at what you do, and for this client, my boss, we need the best."

"And who is your boss, Agent Green?"

Green leaned back in his chair with a self-satisfied smile. He'd conducted dozens of job interviews as head of the SSS, and this was the moment when he would bowl them over with the big reveal. "Santa Claus."

Veronica waited a moment for the real answer but nothing else came from Green. "Are you serious? Santa Claus?"

"Yes, Santa Claus!" declared Green, expecting her to be overcome with amazement.

Veronica stared at him, her frustration growing into bright anger. In a huff, she grabbed her coat and left the office.

Green's smile faded. "Wait, where are you going? You're fleeing the interview?" Green leapt from his chair and chased after her. "Miss Snow! Wait!"

Veronica hurried down a long institutional-looking corridor, the sound of her heels echoing as they clacked against the floor. Green raced up to her. She kept a steady pace, ignoring him.

"Miss Snow, please wait," said Green.

"Santa Claus? Do you think I'm a moron?"

"On the contrary, you are one of the smartest people I have ever met."

Veronica slowed slightly at the compliment. "Who are you really, Mr. Green?"

"I told you. I am head of operations for Santa's Secret Service."

Veronica picked up her pace again, laying on thick sarcasm, "I see. That's fantastic. I have an interview with the Easter Bunny and drinks with Batman tomorrow."

"I assure you this is the real deal." Green pulled out a black dress-leather billfold and flashed his badge. The badge emblem was sparkling silver in the shape of a snowflake. Every agent in Santa's Secret Service had a silver snowflake badge and, as in nature, the contours of each snowflake were unique.

Veronica laughed. "Wow, very impressive. I can't believe I was so dumb. I'm supposed to be in Aspen with my fiancé."

"That information wasn't in your file," Green said as if to himself.

Veronica stopped near a set of large double doors, slipping into her thick coat. "I was enticed up here on Christmas Eve with the promise of a salary beyond my wildest dreams and the chance to do something amazing. You were vouched for. Wait, did Beyoncé put you up to this?"

"Who's Beyoncé?"

Veronica stared at him for a minute, waiting for him to break. When she realized that wasn't going to happen she threw her hands in the air. "Santa Claus? You've wasted my time." Veronica pushed through the double doors into the cold night.

Green followed.

The night air was crisp and the moon glimmered off the snow as Veronica looked around for her escape route. "Which way to the landing strip, Mr. Green?"

"Miss Snow, you've come all this way. All I ask is a few minutes of your time to hear what I have to say. I promise it will be worth it."

"You have as long as it takes you to walk me to the plane."

"That's all I need. This way." Green pointed and Veronica quickly moved along a snowy path behind several large buildings as Green pursued her.

"Is this the way to the plane?" called Veronica over her shoulder.

"Take a left!" yelled Green as he caught up with her.

Veronica veered left, maintaining her pace.

"Just a little further. I really do understand how you feel, Miss Snow. When I was first recruited, it was hard for me to believe in all of this."

"All of what? Santa Claus and the North Pole? I'm too old to believe in all of *that*, Mr. Green."

Green laughed.

"What's so funny?"

"The big guy, he always says you're never too old to believe."

"Big guy? I suppose you mean Santa?" Veronica waved her hand, dismissing Green.

Veronica jumped back as Cody Allred, a gruff-looking man in dirt-covered overalls, ran directly in front of them with a team of men dressed like stable hands.

"Everything all right, Cody?" asked Green.

"Nothing we can't handle, sir," Cody said, panting. "Bulb's got himself stuck on the roof."

Green knew that this could be the perfect situation to introduce Veronica to some of the magic of the North Pole. "I think you'll want to see this, Miss Snow," said Green. He gestured toward Cody. "Lead on, Cody."

Cody hurried forward and Green let Veronica step in front of him. They moved past a large hangar.

"He's only just learned to fly and I'm not sure how he got out. Poor little guy," said Cody.

Green saw Veronica shake her head, annoyed. He was quickly losing her. He needed to show her something special. And fast.

They rounded the corner of the hangar. Cody pointed up toward the top of a large toy factory. "See?"

Green watched as Veronica looked up. A small reindeer with a flickering blue nose skittered on the roof, each of its legs seemingly with a mind of its own, dangerously close to the edge.

Green watched as Veronica saw Bulb and was stunned. He could tell she was trying to process the scene before her. She'd stopped walking toward the airfield, and that was just the opening he needed.

"Cody, this is Miss Veronica Snow," Green said. "And Miss Snow, this is Cody Allred, lead caretaker of Santa's reindeer."

Cody tipped his hat to Veronica. "Ma'am."

Veronica, a look of confusion on her face, watched Cody's team on top of the roof secure Bulb in a large blanket. There was no doubt that Bulb was an actual living animal, and if his nose was a fake, it was a brilliant fake, but there was only one way he could have made it to the roof. "Flying reindeer?" whispered Veronica, unable to look away from Bulb.

"Yes," said Green. He stepped closer to her. "Veronica, was there ever a time in your life when you believed in Santa Claus?"

Veronica thought for a second. She looked at Cody, who looked back, earnest, willing her to believe. "Yes," Veronica said slowly, turning toward Green.

"That's the person I need you to be for the next few minutes."

Cody's men brought Bulb down from the roof as Veronica watched. "Is he going to be okay?" she asked.

"Oh sure, he's just not used to flying at night," said Cody, looking to Green, becoming his co-conspirator in revealing their world to Veronica. Green nodded at him.

"Would you like to see the rest of them, ma'am?" Cody asked.

Veronica nodded, clearly dumbfounded, but Green knew there was a part of her that was coming slowly back to life: The part that was alive when she was a child, the part that couldn't sleep on Christmas Eve, the part that wrote letters to Santa Claus and made milk and cookies for him, the part that *believed*.

Green and Cody led Veronica into the area where reindeer were kept in a large, comfortable stable with two rows of pens. One of the rows was empty. Their plaques read: Rudolph, Dasher, Dancer, Prancer, Vixen, Comet, Cupid, Donner, and Blitzen.

The pens in the other row housed reindeer as well and they were all present. Their plaques read: Tinsel, Powder, Racer, Flurry, Astro, Jupiter, Snowball, and Meteor.

Veronica walked along the pens, touching the nameplates to the empty stalls with her hand. "Comet . . . Cupid . . . Donner . . . ," she said to herself, in awe, unable to keep from grinning.

Cody opened one of the pens, letting out one of the reindeer. "Okay, fella, there's a pretty lady I want you to meet."

Veronica reached out her hand to pet the reindeer. She noticed its head had a harness around it that held peculiar leather covering over its nose. "Why does he wear that muzzle?"

"Oh, no, ma'am, that's no muzzle, that's for protection. He could blind you. That nose is bright enough to cut through the thickest fog!"

Cody loosened the cover, allowing a small peek. The reindeer's nose radiated an intense, brilliant shade of emerald green.

Veronica stepped back. "How did you do that?"

"We didn't," said Green. "They get that shine from flying through the Northern Lights."

Veronica stared in childlike wonder. "But, doesn't Rudolph have a red nose?" She asked, at once aware of the absurdity of her question, but also of its absolute relevance.

"This isn't Rudolph, ma'am," said Cody. "Rudy and the boys are out with Mr. Claus this evening. This is Tinsel, leader of the B-team. They're trained to do everything the A-team does if something, heaven forbid, ever went bad."

"And they can . . ." Veronica looked up.

Cody laughed. "Fly? You betcha!" He gestured toward the ceiling. "Up, Tinsel, up!"

Tinsel slowly lifted into the air. Veronica stepped back, her eyes wide. A smile crept over her lips as Green watched her. He'd known that once Veronica had seen the reindeer that he'd have her. His ploy was working and though he knew that she most likely couldn't believe what she was seeing, as she saw the reindeer hovering off the ground, he knew it was starting to become real for her.

Cody gestured Tinsel back to the ground and rewarded him with a treat.

Green caught himself staring at Veronica again. He quickly looked away, trying to remain professional as Veronica continued to look on in amazement. Green walked over and placed a hand on her elbow. He led her to the opposite end of the stable, near the rear door.

"I'm about to show you a world that most people only dream of. Once you've experienced this place, I promise, you'll never want to leave."

"Okay," said Veronica, still in a daze.

"Are you ready?" asked Green.

Veronica, staring straight ahead, nodded.

Green opened the door.

CHAPTER THREE

Green and Veronica walked into a magical view of the North Pole village. It was everything that Veronica had imagined as a child. The houses and buildings looked like ones she'd built out of gingerbread with her father as a young girl. The tiny Swiss chalets and cottages were lined with intricate white picket fences, decorated with elongated wreaths. The pine trees were dressed with tinsel, popcorn, and lights. There were colorful lights everywhere and every door had a wreath displayed. Snow rested perfectly on rooftops and windowsills. Everywhere she looked were the brightest greens and warmest reds she had ever seen.

She looked up. The sky was filled with a dancing stream of red and green, much like the colors of the village. Though Veronica had heard of the Northern Lights and seen pictures, nothing could have prepared her for the sight before her eyes that night. It was a spectacular light show, as captivating as any fireworks display.

"Welcome to the North Pole," said Green.

Hundreds of people were gathered in the village square, anticipating something, looking up into the night sky. The sheer breadth of the most ornate Christmas display come to life overwhelmed Veronica. There were giant candy canes and snowmen everywhere. And everything seemed to glow as if illuminated by some unseen light source. "I don't believe it," she said.

"You've always believed. You've just forgotten," said Green.

Green and Veronica approached the large crowd. As Veronica looked closer she could tell that in addition to people from all walks of life, there were smaller people with pointed ears who stood about three feet tall. "Are those elves?"

"Yes," said Green. "And leprechauns."

"Leprechauns, at the North Pole?"

"When we're short staffed in the toy factory we'll hire leprechauns to pick up the slack. They don't get along that well though, elves and leprechauns."

"Elves are real?"

"I know. It's weird, but yes," said Green.

A handsome SSS agent, who appeared to be in his late twenties, approached Green. "Everything is set, sir. The Beard is making his final approach. He'll touch down in T-minus 90 seconds."

"How's security, Agent Winters?" asked Green.

"Tight as a polar bear's tookus, sir. Except for that." Winters pointed toward a rowdy leprechaun doing a drunken Irish jig. He was bumping into people and out of control. "But don't worry. I've got it handled."

Winters spoke into his candy cane pin and moments later two SSS agents Tasered the unruly leprechaun from behind, dragging him back into the crowd and out of sight.

"Agent Winters, meet Veronica Snow. She may be our new PR man—I mean woman—person!"

Winters and Veronica shook hands.

"Miss Snow, this is my right hand man, Agent Isaac Winters."

"Welcome to the Pole, ma'am."

"Thank you," said Veronica.

Winters turned to Green. "Not a bad night, sir. The big guy made record time."

"How does he do it?" asked Veronica. "How does he deliver all the presents in just one night?"

"Excuse me." Winters stepped away, speaking into his candy cane pin. "All agents, I want a status update."

Veronica looked at Green, her question still on the table. "Okay, Miss Snow, you've asked the million dollar question. And the answer is that Santa does it with a bit of magic and a bit of technology."

Veronica scrunched her nose, not quite buying Green's answer.

Green continued, "Over time, Mr. Claus befriended some of the most brilliant minds in history, men like Nikola Tesla. They helped him create the Time Expander, a device that can freeze time. Pretty simple, huh?"

"Uh, not really," said Veronica.

"Yeah, I don't actually know how it works either."

Veronica laughed and shook her head. She was about to say something when the crowd cheered as Santa's sleigh approached from the horizon. The sleigh, pulled by Santa's reindeer, was resplendent moving through the Northern Lights, hovering, gliding, magical.

Veronica looked up with wonder in her eyes. She reached out, grabbing Green's hand. Green jumped and looked down.

"This is really real," said Veronica.

Green was still looking down at their entwined hands. "It is. Really real." Green smiled.

The reindeer pulled Santa's sleigh into the center of the gathering, landing gently. All of the gathered elves and people rushed toward it, welcoming Santa home.

Winters and Arnold Black, a clean-cut, impossibly skinny agent in his forties, led other agents as they surrounded the perimeter of the sleigh, acting as crowd control. Black kept stealing glances over at Green and Veronica.

Veronica stood by, enthralled as Santa reached down and held up his red velvet bag, which was empty, the symbol that all the gifts had been delivered. The crowd yelled and shouted out with glee as an assistant took the bag from Santa to be stored. Stable hands worked to free the reindeer from their harnesses, feeding them bits of apple and carrots.

Santa disembarked from his sleigh and walked over to Rudolph. He patted Rudolph's head and gently removed his harness. "Well done, my friend."

Cody approached Rudolph and secured the leather guard over his red nose.

"Are you ready to meet him?" Green asked Veronica.

"Now?" she asked. Veronica was suddenly self-conscious; she looked down at her hand still in Green's. She let go and adjusted her hair.

Green was disappointed that they were no longer holding hands, but he loved seeing the look of anticipation and joy on her face. "Of course, stay with me."

Santa walked through the crowd, the folks gathered there to greet him well aware of just how tired he was after the long night of work. They cleared a path and Santa approached the mini gondola lift that would take him over the homes up to the icy bluff where his grand lodge stood overlooking the North Pole village. The lodge was a large wooden structure that resembled an old style Viking castle with hand-carved designs and multiple gables and balconies that lent Santa a view of the expanse of the North Pole and the nearby territories, each with its own special history.

Green and Veronica weren't far behind. Veronica kept her distance behind Green. She was hesitant and not really sure if she belonged.

Santa nodded to an SSS agent, who opened the door to one of the mini gondolas. Santa gestured for Green to come with him. Green led Veronica over and they got in the gondola with Santa.

Veronica stared in awe. Santa didn't notice her as he was waving to the crowd as the gondola rose up the short line to a massive terrace in front of the lodge.

Mrs. Claus and a few housekeepers greeted Santa at the terrace as he got off the gondola. Green and Veronica stood a respectful ways back, waiting for their turn to say hello, but giving the Clauses their privacy.

Santa hugged Mrs. Claus, then turned and walked to the railing and looked down at the large crowd still gathered there. "Well, my friends, please go home to your families! Merry Christmas to all, and to all a good night!"

Behind him, three elves rang the North Pole Christmas bells, signaling the Christmas holiday at the Pole. The crowd let out three loud cheers in unison before dispersing to celebrate.

Santa turned back to Mrs. Claus and they headed toward the lodge. "You must be exhausted. Dinner's on the table," said Mrs. Claus as she embraced Santa. "Welcome home, dear."

"It's good to be back," replied Santa. Santa stopped and put his arms around his wife. He gave Mrs. Claus a kiss.

Mrs. Claus looked past Santa and saw Green. "Don't think that I don't see you there, Noel! You're going to help us eat all of this food. I won't have you spending Christmas alone . . . again."

Green, looking a little embarrassed, glanced at Veronica. "It's always Christmas up here," said Green. He turned back to Mrs. Claus. "Of course I'll stay for dinner."

As Santa walked inside, he took off his boots and removed his large red coat, which he handed to one of the housekeepers. The housekeeper quickly took the coat to a sterilized rejuvenation chamber just off of the living room, where it would remain until the following year.

Santa wore a Coca-Cola T-shirt. "Good work this evening, Agent Green. Thanks for your help with the McKenzie rascals."

"Don't mention it, sir. Looks like another year without incident."

"Thanks to you, Noel. And who is this lovely lady?"

"Oh, yes, Mr. Claus, meet Veronica Snow," said Green. "She came here to interview for the PR position."

Veronica stepped forward as one of the housekeepers took her coat. "It's a pleasure to meet you, Mr. Claus."

"Please, call me Santa. I don't know why Noel insists on calling me Mr. Claus."

"Out of respect, sir," said Green.

Santa rubbed his beard. "Hmm, Veronica Snow?" Santa pulled out an iPad Air and opened up his Naughty & Nice App. "Mrs. Claus got me an iPad Air for Christmas, and oh how I love it. I can access the entire Naughty and Nice Lists with this. Here we are,

Veronica Snow, on the Nice List. Just barely, though!" Santa gave her a wink and smiled.

Veronica blushed.

"Welcome to the North Pole, Veronica," said Santa. "We're so happy to have you. You're going to love it here. It's the happiest place on Earth."

Veronica gave Green a slight look of apprehension.

"He's been using that a lot longer than Disney," Green whispered to Veronica. "He claims they stole it from him." Green turned to Santa. "Just so you know, sir, she hasn't actually accepted the job yet."

"Oh? Well, I hope you'll stay for dinner."

Green quickly interjected. "She can't, sir, she's late for drinks with Batman."

"Batman?" asked Santa.

Green winked at Veronica, who shrugged it off.

"I'd love to," said Veronica.

Green and Veronica sat at a large dining table along with Mr. and Mrs. Claus. An abundance of food remained: turkeys, hams, four kinds of rolls, eight types of jellies, candied yams, mashed potatoes, green bean casserole, and, as Santa insisted every year, a large Chicago-style sausage pizza. There was enough food for multiple families.

"Thank you, Mrs. Claus," said Green. "That was wonderful. I'm stuffed."

"Hope you don't think you're done, Green. Eat up!" Santa passed Green a large bowl of fluffy mashed potatoes and gave him a stern look. Green slowly put more on his plate, regretting that he'd been roped into another dinner at Santa's home. He'd have to do extra miles on his run tomorrow.

Santa turned to Veronica. "And what about you, my dear? Did you get enough?"

Veronica had never eaten more in her entire life. "Oh yes, thank you. I couldn't eat another bite."

"I bet Jay-Z never fed you this well when you were working for him, did he?" asked Santa.

Veronica laughed, though she was struck with the notion that Santa seemed to know quite a lot about her.

"Santa, can I ask you a question?" asked Veronica.

"Of course, my dear," said Santa.

"Do you remember every girl and boy that you deliver toys to?"

Santa considered the question. "No," he said, taking another moment, "but I remember my favorites. I remember that you asked me for a Cabbage Patch Kid in 1989."

Veronica smiled. "That's right, and I got her too, Tiffany Marie. Oh my gosh, I loved her so much! You do remember. That was one of my most favorite Christmases ever."

"What about you, Noelie? What was one of your most favorite Christmases?" asked Mrs. Claus.

Green remained quiet. He stared at the mashed potatoes that he'd sculpted into a snowman.

"Noel?" prompted Mrs. Claus.

"I'm sorry, Mrs. Claus," said Green. "I don't really have a lot of good Christmas memories."

Mrs. Claus fought to keep her emotions in check; the notion that anyone anywhere at anytime could not have positive memories of Christmas was such a sad thing for her to hear. "Oh, my dear, I'm so sorry."

Santa was looking right at Green. He opened his mouth to say something, but Green interjected.

"Well, this has been a lovely dinner, Mrs. Claus. We had better get going, though. I still have to debrief the security team." Green stood quickly wanting to get out of there before it got even more personal.

"It *is* Christmas Eve, Noel," said Santa. "Let them have the rest of the night off."

"Sorry, sir, you know we can't take *any* night off."

"I'm sorry," Veronica said with a soft voice, "but all this security, the SSS, I wouldn't think you would need protection, Santa. Who in their right mind would want to hurt you?"

"Oh, don't worry about it, dear," said Santa. "It's just a tiny precaution. I'm not in any danger. There are a few Naughties out there, but nothing to worry about, ho, ho, ho. Although Agent Green might disagree with me."

"There is always a threat somewhere. And I need to get back to it."

Green helped Veronica to her feet. They hugged Santa and Mrs. Claus and said their goodbyes.

The door shut behind Green and Veronica, and Mrs. Claus put her arms around Santa. "She's a pretty girl. Do you think Noel noticed?"

"I don't think Noel notices anything." Santa laughed and gave Mrs. Claus a hug.

CHAPTER FOUR

Far away from the North Pole, on the opposite end of the globe, a large fortress stood within the side of a giant mountain of ice and rock. Stalactites and stalagmites surrounded the front of the fortress, like teeth.

Inside one of the rooms, a massive desk sat in front of a fireplace that nearly filled the wall. The fire burned blue, the heat held at bay by a metallic encasing that resembled the jaws of a wolf.

Perched behind the desk was Cole, a very thin elf, with dry lips that were pinched together in a permanent scowl. He was dressed entirely in black and his fingernails were filed to sharp points. A patchy, prickly beard covered his pale face, and dark circles hung underneath his icy blue eyes.

He stood up and went to the window, looking out on a beautiful sunny day. Several penguins waddled by in the snow outside. "I hate the South Pole," said Cole.

French doors at the opposite side of the room swung open. Standing there was Frostbite, a lanky human with albinism also dressed in black. He had spiked white hair and piercing blue eyes.

"What is it, you creepy albino?" asked Cole.

"He's here. Would you like me to show him in, sir?"

"Yes, you pinhead! And tell Ivy I need some more rotten milk. The last cup was too fresh."

Frostbite nodded and bowed slightly before gesturing to someone just beyond the door. Agent Black entered the room as Frostbite left.

"Come in, Black," said Cole. "You must be tired from your travels."

Black sat in a chair in front of Cole's desk.

A woman dressed in a French maid's outfit with an elfish twist entered the room with a silver tray. Ivy was Cole's human girlfriend. In her early twenties and with dark black hair, she could have passed for "goth chic" had she been at a college campus and not Cole's lair in the South Pole.

A pitcher of rotten, sour milk sat atop her tray. Ivy bent down to Cole's level as she poured the curdled milk into a large mug on Cole's desk, clumps and liquid dropping into the mug. On the mug was a picture of Santa's hat with an X over it.

Ivy turned to Black. "Rotten milk?" she asked him.

"Uh, no thanks, I'm trying to quit."

"Thank you, my dear. Now get out of here," said Cole.

Ivy gave a small curtsey and headed for the door.

"I appreciate you coming all the way to the South Pole, Agent Black. Good bad people are hard to find."

"Thank you, sir," said Black.

"So, report. How are things up north?" asked Cole.

"When I left they were congratulating themselves on pulling off another disgusting display of gift giving."

"Well, I hope they enjoyed themselves because it's the last time they'll ever celebrate Christmas like that." Cole laughed, sinister, full of menace. He went on for a few moments.

Cole stopped laughing and glared at Black.

"What?" Black was afraid. He'd seen that cold, intense look in Cole's eyes before. It never led to anything enjoyable. "I'm not really a big laugher."

Cole stared at Black for a moment, then smiled. "That's what I like about you; you're all business."

"Yes, sir."

"But things will really be different up there next year. Very different," said Cole, chuckling to himself before taking another big gulp of rotten milk. He wiped clumps of rancid milk off his beard.

CHAPTER FIVE

Green and Veronica walked through the village square. The celebrations were over, and they were the only ones outside.

"Back in the day—this was before my time—Santa was a big pipe smoker. Every time he was shown in the press, he had his pipe. A few years back, your predecessor decided that smoking wasn't good for Santa's image. So he quit; no more pipe."

"Well that seems like it was a good idea. Wasn't it?" asked Veronica.

"Well, sure, we know that it wasn't a good thing for Santa to be smoking. But at the time, losing his pipe was like changing his suit to yellow."

Veronica laughed. "Now *that* would be a big deal."

"I know it. My point is that millions of children look up to him and we take that very seriously. Every change, no matter how subtle, must be given the utmost care. It's why we don't make very many and it's why we need the best public relations rep there is."

"What happened to the last one?" asked Veronica.

"The Norman Rockwell campaign was basically the last real good idea he had. He was just a little behind the times, I'm not sure he even knows what the Internet is."

Veronica laughed.

"Mr. Claus needs someone more current, someone who can handle the modern political landscape. We want Santa very much in the public square, promoting Christmas and his message of hope and joy."

Green led Veronica to a large wooden structure. He opened the door and entered a giant assembly plant that was empty and quiet. Their voices echoed in the large space.

"This is one of our factories where the toys are made," said Green.

Veronica stopped by one of the conveyer belts and saw a brand-new PlayStation 4.

"Santa's elves make PlayStations?" she asked.

"Nowadays kids are asking for PS4s and iPads, not hop-a-long boots and rocking horses. Major companies get overwhelmed during the holiday season and send us the raw components. Our elves put them together. Times have gotten more advanced and our elves have gotten more sophisticated."

"So, you mean Steve Jobs would come here and show them how to assemble iPads?" Veronica asked, smiling.

"Actually, yes. Before his death, Steve Jobs was one of our biggest supporters."

Veronica laughed. Green didn't.

"Really?" Veronica asked.

"Yes, and when you decide to work here, you will be meeting quite a few leaders of major companies and countries all over the world."

"Wow." Veronica paused and pondered. "So if elves make the toys, why are there no elves on Santa's security team?"

"Would you feel safe with a tiny little elf as your bodyguard? Elves make toys; that is what they do best."

"I know why you brought me up here on this night. I thought it was strange to be doing an interview on Christmas Eve. Who does that? But it's the best night of the year up here, isn't it?"

"Nothing can beat seeing Santa's sleigh coming home through the Northern Lights," said Green. "It's a great deal closer."

"You made a very convincing pitch," Veronica said as she looked around at the massive factory.

Green watched her; he was having a hard time keeping his eyes off her. "I remember the day that I was standing here for the first time. I've never forgotten that this is somewhat surreal."

Veronica nodded. "It is."

"So, do you want the job?" Green asked.

Veronica contemplated for a moment, then smiled.

"Just say it," said Green.

Veronica laughed, overcome by the moment. "Yes."

Green and Veronica sat in a small booth in the corner of the Northern Lights Tavern. The place was filled with elves, people, and a few leprechauns celebrating another year of hard work. Some of them were singing karaoke.

Green handed Veronica a small ring box.

"But Agent Green, we just met," Veronica laughed.

"Wait, what? That's not what I meant." In a panic Green quickly opened the box, exposing a small candy cane pin.

"Easy, Turbo, I was joking," Veronica said as she took the pin from the box.

"All essential staff at the Pole have one. We use these to communicate and track each other, which is really important when you're back on the mainland."

Realization settled over Veronica's face. "The mainland! Oh, I've said yes to the job and I haven't talked to my fiancé about any of this." She shook her head. "Wow, that probably says something, huh?"

"Does what say . . . what? I'm sorry, I don't think I understand the question."

"Nothing, I'm sorry. I shouldn't have said that." Veronica looked away as Green took a sip of hot chocolate.

After an awkward silence, Veronica smiled and looked back at Green. "What about you? You ever go home, back in the real world?"

"I assure you Miss Snow, this place is as real as anywhere. All of our agents are on rotation. They get several months off during the year."

"Yes, but I asked about you," Veronica said. "Do you have family you go home to?"

Green put his hands up, calling attention to the setting. "I do have a family: a jolly man, his lovable wife, and about six thousand elves." Green's speech was rushed and there was something melancholic about the way he spoke about Santa and Mrs. Claus.

Veronica reached out and put her hand over his. "Well, they're lucky to have you."

Green looked down at her hand and then up at her eyes. Veronica held his gaze for a moment before looking away and removing her hand from his. It took Green a moment longer before he finally looked away as well.

CHAPTER SIX

The next six months flew by in a blur. Green oversaw security at the Pole in preparation for next Christmas while Veronica settled into her new job. It was a lot more work than she'd expected. She had soon realized the challenge in running public relations for a man who most people believed wasn't real—and who wouldn't ever confirm his existence.

This fact had led to the one argument Veronica had with Santa. She couldn't figure out why he didn't just come out and go on Fallon or Kimmel and prove to the world that he existed, that reindeer could fly, and that the magic of the North Pole was very real. Santa had insisted that the element of belief in something unseen was the most important aspect of what he did, that it was the essence of hope, and it made Christmas magical. If the curtain were pulled back, so to speak, some of that would be lost. At least that's what Santa had told her. Veronica had decided not to press the point and went to work trying to help Santa keep up with the modern world.

The biggest obstacle was the current movement to stop referring to Christmas as, well, Christmas. *Happy Holidays*, *Winter Celebration*, and *Seasons Greetings* were all replacing *Merry Christmas*.

Many of the largest retailers had stopped posting Christmas signs in their stores, and some towns had banned Christmas songs from being sung on school property.

Santa was surprisingly understanding of this as Veronica worked to keep Santa in the public eye. She learned that the love for Santa Claus was still there, out in the world. In fact, it was pervasive. He was above the controversy over the word *Christmas*, which she learned was politically motivated by a small minority. It wasn't really something that registered with the general public at all.

Santa explained to Veronica that the true message of Christmas was really about giving, gifts, and the hope they can inspire in others. Veronica tailored her public relations platform to focus on Santa, the North Pole, generosity, and the tradition of gift giving. And it was a huge success. She was even able to get the words *Merry Christmas* approved for use in the United States Congress. She'd put a special emphasis on the Macy's Thanksgiving Day Parade, ensuring it would be a very special event that year.

As tradition held at the North Pole, summer was when things shut down and many of the SSS agents and human North Pole employees returned to their homes on the mainland. Veronica was anxious to get back to the life that she'd left behind when she took the job with Santa Claus and to implement those elements of her PR campaign that could only be done in person. Her fiancé had been understanding but skeptical. She still hadn't told him whom she was really working for. How he handled that news would decide if they still had a future together.

All of these thoughts were on Veronica's mind as she prepared to take a plane back home. The sun was low and hordes of other people were preparing to leave as well. They stood by as elves loaded luggage onto several airplanes parked on the North Pole landing strip. It was somewhat comical to watch the elves handling human-sized luggage, but Veronica had learned not to laugh at them. It was easy; their work ethic was impressive. Agent Black and other SSS agents helped coordinate the flow.

Santa and Mrs. Claus were bundled up, since it was always cold at the North Pole, saying their good-byes. Green and Winters escorted Veronica to the landing strip, carrying her belongings for her. Veronica stopped at the Clauses.

"Well, Miss Snow," said Santa, "you've done great work. We'll see you next season."

"Thank you, Santa," said Veronica.

Veronica hugged Mrs. Claus. "Goodbye, my dear. Be sure to send us a wedding invite."

Winters flashed a quick look at Green, who ignored him.

"I will," said Veronica. "Take good care of these boys."

Veronica turned and headed for her plane with Green and Winters in tow. Green handed her luggage off to an attendant.

"Well, this is it," said Green.

"It is," said Veronica. "I'll be seeing you."

Green went to shake Veronica's hand as she went in for a hug. They awkwardly changed to match each other's movement.

Winter's cringed at the exchange. "Whoops," he said.

Green and Veronica gave each other a quick hug.

"Bye," said Veronica. She turned and hurried to the plane. The attendant climbed in after her and closed the door.

"Off to see the fiancé," said Winters. "You think she'll be back?"

"She'll be back," said Green, his eyes never leaving Veronica's plane until it was safely in the air and out of sight.

CHAPTER SEVEN

Cole stood in the grand hall of his fortress. He was in front of a mirror checking his appearance, though it was unclear why he did this as his black clothing, severe grooming, and sinister disposition rarely changed. Behind him hung a banner that read 'OPERATION HUMBUG'.

Cole watched as Ivy pushed in a rolling ladder. She climbed up and started to hang a smaller banner. Cole tilted his head, watching her. The banner unfurled and revealed the words *Mission Accomplished*.

Cole stomped his foot. "Not yet! I'm surrounded by a bunch of snow blowers!"

"I just wanted to see how it looks," said Ivy.

"It *looks* like you're a moron, my dear," Cole muttered to himself.

Agent Black entered as Ivy took the banner down.

"Welcome back, Agent Black," said Cole. "What word do you have from the North?"

"Not much to report sir. The Northies still don't expect any danger."

"Those sugar-coated buffoons!" Cole cackled.

"Security is minimal, nothing we can't handle. They're not ready for real action. They've hired a new girl to their staff, a very attractive girl. Green seems to like her."

"Pffft, Green! What a mama's boy. Good work, Black," said Cole.

"We're all set for Operation Humbug," declared Black.

Cole picked up his quill pen and circled a date on his desk

calendar: November 12 of the current year. On that date was written OPERATION HUMBUG.

Cole paced in front of Black and Ivy. "Yes, yes, it's all as I planned. Those gift-loving fools have tasted their final figgy pudding."

Black and Ivy exchanged a curious glance.

"What?" demanded Cole.

"What's figgy pudding?" asked Ivy.

Cole laughed. "Are you kidding me? It's a line from a song!"

"You don't have to get mad at me," said Ivy.

Cole walked over to Ivy. She stepped back, her gait faltering as she kept her eyes on him.

Cole flew forward and put his arms around her before she could slink away. He was about half her height so she bent down to his embrace. Hugging wasn't something that came natural to Cole. That, combined with their difference in height, made the exchange very strange.

"Uh, do you want me to leave?" asked Black.

"Quiet down, Black, I'm having a moment," said Cole.

Black stood still, feeling awkward but afraid to leave.

Cole ran his hand along Ivy's cheek. "Listen to me, dear. Come next winter, no one will ever hear that song again. We will write new songs! The fat man and his systematic programming of the children of the world will be nothing but a snowy memory! And the children will sing about me, and what I am about to do."

Ivy nodded. "But you won't hurt anyone, right?"

"Sure, sure, it's all going to be fine," said Cole, the malevolent gleam in his eye hinting otherwise.

Cole hugged Ivy close and winked at Black over her shoulder.

Black tried to wink back, but it was a maneuver he'd never quite mastered and he just looked like he had something in his eyes.

Cole shook his head.

PART TWO

CHAPTER EIGHT

The toy factory at the North Pole bustled with activity. It was November and the elves were back at work, assembling toys, electronics, and various gifts, all in preparation for another Christmas Eve. Conveyor belts carried finished products to different areas of the factory. From there the toys were moved to massive warehouses where they would be separated by country and then state, province, or territory. Three weeks before Christmas the enormous task of wrapping the gifts would begin and continue twenty-four hours a day, six days a week, until December 24.

While these preparations for Christmas were going on all over the Pole, the heads of Santa's key units were assembled around a frosted-glass oval table inside SSS headquarters. The table had intricate stencils in the shape of wreaths. They were in a boardroom with a view of the SSS Command Center.

SSS agents, elves, and other leaders of the Pole were there for the first meeting since all essential staff had returned from their time away. This was an annual meeting that was always well attended, partly because Mrs. Claus was typically ready with a plethora of treats and goodies. There were Christmas tree–shaped donuts, four kinds of cookies, sweet rolls, coffee, hot chocolate, eggnog, orange juice, chocolate milk, and croissants with red and green–striped frosting on them.

Santa sat at the head of the table, polishing off his fourth croissant. Green stood in front of the group as he wrapped up his yearly speech about the importance of security. The others tried to listen as they gorged themselves on the food Mrs. Claus had set before them.

Winters sat near the end of the table with an overflowing plate of treats. He filled a yawn with an entire donut.

"With Christmas only a month and a half away, you'll notice more of our agents arriving over the coming weeks ahead. We've got a lot of training before the holiday season," said Green.

Veronica hurried into the room, flustered, carrying an armload of binders and paperwork.

Green watched Veronica take the empty seat next to Santa. It was the first time he had seen her since she'd left before the summer. He couldn't help but check her ring finger. It was bare.

"Welcome back, Miss Snow," said Green.

Veronica forced a smile and gave an awkward wave.

"If there's nothing else, we'll dismiss. Mr. Claus has a busy day ahead."

"Thank you, Agent Green," said Santa. Santa turned to Veronica. "Welcome back. How was your break?"

"Fine, great," said Veronica, brushing off the question.

Santa paused. He could tell something was wrong, but it wasn't the time or the place to address it. Santa gave her a quick pat on her hand and left the room, trailed by a line of elves and assistants.

The rest of the group took their time standing. Each of them filled their plates again as they headed out of the room. Green watched Veronica as she shook hands and greeted many of the people. She looked over and locked eyes with Green.

"How was your time back in 'the real world'?" Green asked.

"Hi, Noel," said Veronica. "Sorry I'm late. I missed everything."

"That's all right. Agent Burke can fill you in."

"Well, I'll see you around?"

Green nodded and Veronica gathered her things and followed Santa out of the room. Green stared after her.

"Someone broke off their engagement," said Winters.

"What?" asked Green, turning away from the door.

"Yup. Agent Collins heard that Veronica canceled the wedding this summer. The fiancé didn't like her taking the job up here. I heard the guy's a real snow job."

In the official SSS gym, Green and Winters pranced around in a boxing ring, sparring. Green insisted that all SSS agents stay in top shape and train year round. He led by example, often pulling Winters into long workouts.

"Put the pieces together. She takes this job far away, doesn't even consult the guy. No way he's okay with that," said Winters as they exchanged light jabs.

"You hear all of this at the nail salon?" asked Green. "You sound like one of the women on *The Real Housewives of Beverly Hills.*"

WHAP! Winters punched Green square in the face, knocking him on his back.

Continuing their training and conversation outside, Green and Winters were decked out in snow gear. They crawled under barbed wire, making their way through an intricate obstacle course. Springing to their feet, they moved to the next station.

"Everybody in the North Pole knows you've got a thing for her," said Winters. "I'm starting to wonder if you're all wrapping and no present."

"Everybody in the North Pole needs to stop worrying about my packaging and focus on their jobs."

"All I'm saying is that I've seen you together. There's some real chemistry between you two," said Winters as they maneuvered over a tall wall.

Green and Winters swung over an icy pit of water as simulated explosions ripped through the snow all around them.

Green and Winters glided on cross-country skis across a wide snow-field, rifles flung over their backs. They stopped at the edge of a trail and pulled out their rifles.

"I've seen the way you look at her. The only thing that held you back was her fiancé, and he's out of the picture," said Winters, taking aim with his rifle. "It would be better if the SSS gave us real guns, not these lame Freeze Rays."

Winters fired his rifle, which emitted a bolt of green lightning, striking a target planted in the snowfield.

"You know the rules, no lethal force. That comes straight from the big guy. Besides, there's never been an incident that would justify it."

Green fired his rifle, hitting the target with dead accuracy. He took pride in his marksmanship. Though lethal force was forbidden in the SSS, Green aimed to be prepared should the day ever arrive when he would have no choice but to use it.

They slung their rifles over their shoulders and took off on their skis, stopping at a bluff overlooking the North Pole Village.

Green looked over at Winters. "You really think we have chemistry?"

Veronica stood outside the reindeer stable with Cody, feeding carrots to Bulb. It had been almost a year since she had last seen Bulb, and he was close to a full-grown reindeer now, with antlers and a still-flickering blue nose.

Green and Winters drove past on a snowmobile. Green's eyes followed Veronica as he rode past.

Winters leaned over to Green. "If you don't make your move, I'm going to. I'll show you how it's done. Winters and Snow go great together."

"You're a real low-hanging ornament, Winters," said Green.

Veronica stood at the end of a long line in the dining hall of the North Pole Community Center, talking on her cell phone. Green approached, getting in line behind her.

"That's unacceptable. . . . Well, just go back to the drawing board . . . . Call me when you have some ideas we can use." Veronica clicked off her phone in a huff.

Veronica saw Green and shook her head.

"That was Coca-Cola. They want to put Santa on a beach with a bunch of scantily clad women running around."

"Classy," said Green.

"Exactly." Veronica sighed. "Well, Agent Noel Green, I see you've managed to keep the North Pole in one piece for the rest of us."

"I wasn't alone. You didn't think I was here by myself, did you?"

"It's a joke, Agent Green," said Veronica, shaking her head at Green's continued lack of humor.

"Oh, right . . . Santa is doing a walk-through of the main toy assembly plant," said Green. "I was wondering if you'd like to attend."

"Yes. I'd like that."

"Great! After lunch we can go together. Well, not together, together. I just meant that you and I could go at the same time."

They came to a pile of trays. Veronica picked one up, smiling. "I know what you meant, silly. That would be fine. Why don't we share a table?"

Upon hearing this Green nervously knocked over the pile of trays, scattering them across the floor. Green bent down and picked up a single tray. He looked up at Veronica and shrugged, trying to play it cool. "Sure," he said.

Back at SSS headquarters, Agent Black walked down a corridor. He looked over his shoulder as he came to a security checkpoint. He placed his hand to a scanner, which read his palm print. The door opened.

Black entered a large surveillance room filled with screens showing different views of the North Pole. He clicked on a few buttons and a view of the toy factory gate appeared on screen.

Black spoke into a tiny handheld radio. "Okay, Frostbite, you're clear."

On the screen, a FED-XMAS delivery truck approached the gates. Black pressed a few buttons and the gates opened.

Inside the FED-XMAS truck, Frostbite sat at the wheel, dressed in the official FED-XMAS uniform. He pulled the truck over by the entry to the toy factory.

Frostbite exited the truck with a package under his arm. He jogged up to the main entrance where an SSS agent was sitting inside of a control booth.

"Dropping off or picking up?" asked the SSS agent.

"Dropping off," said Frostbite, holding up his FED-XMAS identification.

The SSS agent scanned his ID.

Frostbite stood erect, carrying himself with the posture of someone in charge, as they waited for the system to give him clearance. He let out a small sigh of relief as the agent pressed a button and the door opened.

Green and Veronica stood by each other in an elevator in the toy factory coming up from the lower level where the toys were assembled. Green always prepped the elves before Santa visited for his walk-through of the plant. He needed them to remember that Santa's time was precious this time of year and to try not to bother him as he worked.

Green and Veronica were now headed up to the main level to greet Santa. Green looked at her out of the corner of his eye. She glanced over at him and he averted her glance.

"Sh-Boom (Life Could Be A Dream)" by The Crew Cuts played over the speakers in the elevator.

"I love this song," said Green.

The elevator doors opened and Frostbite entered, carrying the package. He stood between Green and Veronica.

Green bopped his head to the music. *"If I could take you to paradise up above,"* he sang along.

Frostbite glanced at Green.

"He loves this song," said Veronica.

The doors opened and Green gestured to Frostbite to exit first. As Frostbite stepped out of the elevator, Green noticed a tiny tattoo on the back of his neck. It was the bottom portion of a compass, with an arrow pointing down to an S.

Frostbite walked through the main area of the toy factory, passing elves at work. He came to an elfin receptionist.

"Dropping off?" asked the receptionist.

"I just need you to sign," said Frostbite as he produced a small, electronic clipboard. The receptionist signed and Frostbite handed her the package. Frostbite made his way toward the exit with a sinister smile on his face.

Green and Veronica stood in the lobby, waiting for Santa Claus. Green was distracted. There was something scratching at his brain, but he couldn't quite place it. He knew that he'd been too focused on Veronica, but there was something about that FED-XMAS deliveryman . . . Green looked up as Santa Claus arrived.

Veronica moved to Santa's side. "Hello, Santa," she said.

"And a hello to you, my dear," said Santa.

Green turned away from them as the thought he'd been searching for became clear in his head. He spoke into his candy cane pin. "This is Agent Green. Was there a scheduled FED-XMAS delivery today?"

Agent Burke's voice came back over Green's earpiece. "That's a negative, sir."

Veronica watched Green, curious, as he barely looked at her, his eyes scanning the area. Something had him worried.

Green moved quickly over to Santa and Veronica. He grabbed both of them and spun them toward the door.

"We have to get out of here now!" shouted Green as he started moving them toward the exit.

"But I thought we had a walk-through planned," said Santa.

"Sir, I don't have time to explain, but you need to get as far away from this place as possible. Go now!"

Green shoved Veronica and Santa out the doorway. They stumbled outside and looked back at Green with confusion.

"Run!" screamed Green as he turned and sprinted back inside.

Green ran into the main operations hub of the factory and approached an elf foreman, Franklin Archer, who wore overalls and a hard hat. Green held up his badge.

"You have to get everybody out of here!"

"What? Why?" asked Archer.

"An explosive device is about to go off!"

"Holy Toledo! Yes sir, right away."

Archer grabbed a telephone on a support column as Green grabbed his hand. "Be calm, we don't need them panicking."

Archer nodded and spoke into the phone. "Attention all workers, this is Foreman Archer, I need everybody to stop what you're doing and calmly exit the factory, immediately!"

Archer turned to Green with the phone still in his hand. "Is there really a bomb in here?" His voice was heard over the loud speaker. Panic erupted amongst the factory workers. Crowds of elves and leprechauns appeared through every doorway and ran for their lives toward the exits.

Green gave Archer a scowl.

"Whoopsy!" exclaimed Archer.

Outside, elves and leprechauns streaked out of the building in droves. Green followed them out and ran into Winters.

"What's going on, sir?" asked Winters.

Green spoke quickly, but calmly. "Winters, I need you to get Mr. Claus to a secure location. Get him away from here."

Green pointed to Veronica and Santa Claus standing clueless in the crowd. Winters signaled and two other agents joined him as he ran toward Santa and Veronica. They moved into a protective formation around them and escorted them away from the building.

Green helped clear the last of the elves and leprechauns out of the building. As he turned to run, the building exploded, throwing Green to the ground. He covered his head as debris fell.

As the explosion ended, Green took a few moments to gather himself. The front of the factory was completely destroyed. Shredded brick and rebar hung from what was left of the structure, dangling like ragged threads from torn fabric. The blast had demolished vehicles near the factory and the flames from the detonation had melted the snow and ice on the ground, leaving a trail of scorched gravel. Green got up and looked over at the others nearby. Everybody seemed to be safe.

Green spotted Archer and ran to him. "Did everyone make it out?"

Archer nodded. "Yes, sir, we have a tight protocol, and I'm always the last to leave. I made sure there wasn't anyone left inside."

"Good man," said Green.

"Who could have done such a thing?" asked Archer.

In the distance, Green saw Frostbite running toward the FED-XMAS truck. "I intend to find out." Green took off running.

Just as Green reached the truck, Frostbite came flying out of the back end on a black snowmobile. He gunned the engine and sped away.

Green frantically scanned the area. He spotted an unattended snowmobile parked outside a workshop. He pinched the candy cane pin on his jacket's lapel and spoke into it as he ran to the snowmobile. "This is Agent Green. I'm following the bombing suspect on snowmobile. We're on the north side of the factory. I need all agents to secure headquarters immediately! And locate Mrs. Claus! The Beard is on lockdown as of right now! Over!"

Green jumped on the snowmobile and took off after Frostbite.

Frostbite careened through a vast expanse of snow and ice. He turned and saw Green was on his heels. Frostbite made a sharp turn onto an embankment. He flew into the air and landed on a plateau.

Green made the same sharp turn and jump. He pulled his Freeze Ray pistol from its holster and fired. Bursts of green lightning shot toward Frostbite, who maneuvered his vehicle away from the oncoming assault.

"We should have real guns!" Green exclaimed.

Frostbite grabbed a tiny bell off his belt and hurled it toward Green. The bell landed in the snow close to Green and exploded.

Green whipped his snowmobile to the side, avoiding another blast and launching off an ice ramp. He sailed through the air and landed next to Frostbite.

Frostbite smashed his snowmobile into Green's. Green slipped off to the side but pulled himself back up, correcting his steering and slamming back into Frostbite's vehicle. They hurtled toward a narrow opening in a glacier wall, just wide enough for one snowmobile.

Green had to slow to allow Frostbite to enter the opening, then swung in behind, following Frostbite into the crevasse. They wove through a maze of ice, their vehicles scraping the frozen-solid walls, friction causing sparks to fly. Green wiped snow and ice from his face as they jostled for position in the tight corridors. There was light up ahead and Frostbite ripped a long icicle free from a ridge as they rocketed out of the maze.

Green hit the throttle up and swooped alongside Frostbite's snowmobile. Frostbite jammed the icicle at Green, ripping through his jacket and shoulder. Green winced in pain.

Frostbite took another bell from his belt; he had a perfect shot at Green, but before he could launch the attack, a blinding green light flashed directly above him. Frostbite flinched and the explosive flew out of his hand, blowing a massive hole in the ice just ahead of Green's snowmobile.

The light radiated from a reindeer's nose before the chasing duo. On the reindeer's back was Winters, who watched in horror as Green's snowmobile crashed through the hole in the weakened ice, sending him into freezing water.

Frostbite accelerated and disappeared behind an icy snow bank.

Winters turned toward Frostbite, but turned back to see Green treading water.

"Go! He's getting away!" shouted Green.

Winters was torn, but knew Green wouldn't last long in the frigid water. Winters pulled the reins and Tinsel swooped down over the hole in the ice, positioning them above Green. Green reluctantly reached up and grabbed Winter's hand, and Winters pulled him from the chilly water.

"Up, Tinsel, up," commanded Winters.

Tinsel and Winters lifted Green out of the water and lowered him onto a snow bank. Green trembled uncontrollably. "The suspect, he's . . ." Green had a hard time speaking through the shivers that racked his body.

"Sit tight, boss. We're going to get you out of here." Winters dismounted Tinsel.

"He's . . . getting away," said Green through chattering teeth.

Winters spoke into his candy cane pin. "North Pole, this is Agent Winters. Send a rescue chopper. Agent Green is down and needs medical attention right away. Over."

Burke's voice came over Winter's earpiece. "Yes, sir. We're on our way. Over."

Winters took off his coat and draped it over Green. "We're going to get you warmed up in a flash."

"They hit the Pole," said Green.

"I know. Just hang on, help's on the way."

"They hit the Pole," Green said again, fatigue, cold, and anguish washing over him.

CHAPTER NINE

Down in the South Pole, Cole entered the kennel area where his flying dogsled team lived. Eight ferocious wolves with glowing red eyes were in their own cages. They had their names on plaques: Phantom, Nightmare, Rogue, Shadow, Grudge, Shriek, Cain, and Diablo.

Cole opened each cage and placed a raw steak inside from his stacked platter.

"Here you go, Phantom," Cole said as he opened the cage housing the biggest wolf. "Daddy's got a nice, juicy steak for you."

Phantom jumped in the air, caught the steak in his mouth, and remained hovering.

At the other end of the kennel was the biggest cage in the room. A giant abominable snowman named Avalanche was locked behind the bars, eight feet tall and covered in white hair. He was crouched in the corner with his head down as Cole approached the cage.

"Wake up, Avalanche! I've got your supper."

Avalanche did not move.

"Get up, you overgrown snow monkey!"

Still nothing.

"Fine!" Cole pelted Avalanche with the steak. Avalanche remained still.

"Do you have any idea how hard it is to get top-quality Angus beef down here? In case you haven't noticed, we're in the South Pole!"

Ivy came in behind Cole. "Be nice to Avalanche," she said.

Cole jumped back, startled. "Darn it, Ivy! Don't go sneaking up on me like that; you almost gave me a heart attack."

"You have to have a heart in order to have a heart attack," said Ivy, absently twirling her hair.

Cole laughed. "Touché, my dear, touché!"

"Frostbite just called in," said Ivy. "He has an update on your Operation Bum Hug or whatever it is."

"Humbug! It's humbug! How many times do I have to tell you?"

Ivy shrugged, spun, and left the room.

Cole entered a large room filled with high-tech surveillance screens and sat at the controls. He pressed some buttons on the control panel next to him.

"Operation Bum Hug . . . where do I find these lowlifes?" Cole muttered to himself.

A large screen on the wall came to life. Frostbite appeared.

"Frostbite. Give me good news. Is that fat 'bowl full of jelly' dead?"

Frostbite looked down. "No, sir."

"What do you mean, no? Is Claus kaput?"

"The toy factory is destroyed, but they evacuated everyone before the explosion," said Frostbite.

"Are you telling me that Operation Bum Hug—Argh! I mean, Humbug—was unsuccessful?"

"I'm afraid so."

"You had one job, you pale freak, one job!" said Cole.

"I'm sorry, sir, I—"

Cole threw his hand on the disconnect button. He sat back, already formulating his Plan B.

CHAPTER TEN

In a Chicago apartment building back in the late 1980s, a young Noel Green finished hanging his stocking over the fireplace. Several of his handmade paper snowflakes and brightly colored cardboard gingerbread men adorned the room, fixed to the walls and counters with Scotch tape as there was not a tree to be found. He hummed "Santa Claus is Coming to Town" as he peeled off more tape and hung hand-colored pictures of Santa Claus and his reindeer he'd cut out of an activity book his mom had given him.

Through a doorway that led to a small kitchenette, Green's mother, Mary, washed dishes. Hard circumstances had worn her down, shielding her once beautiful features.

"Mom, what do reindeers eat?" asked Young Green.

"I don't know, sweetheart. Carrots, I suppose. I'm pretty sure reindeer eat carrots."

"Really? Can I have some for them? I'll leave them on the table with Santa's milk and cookies. I'm sure they get really hungry flying him all over the world."

"Of course, sweetie. I'll make sure we have some by Christmas Eve."

Young Green looked up as his father, Bruce, walked through the front door. He wore a filthy janitor's jumpsuit and was clearly exhausted after another fourteen-hour day.

"Hi, honey," said Mary.

"Did you bring home a tree, dad?" asked Young Green.

"No, son. I told you it wasn't in the cards."

Young Green pouted and kicked at scraps of paper on the floor, leftovers from his crafts. "But I made all these decorations for a tree."

"Sorry, Noel, it's not happening." Bruce dropped into a recliner.

"Bruce, please, he's been working on them all day," said Mary.

Bruce sighed. "Stuff like that is a waste of time, son. Know why?"

"Bruce, don't!" yelled Mary.

"Because Santa Claus isn't real! He's made up by the stooges on Madison Ave."

"That's not true; I know he's real," said Young Green.

"Nope. He isn't. It's a lie and I'm not buying in. Look, I'm not the bad guy. The sooner you realize that no magic man is going to come make your life better, the sooner you can get on with making it better yourself."

"He's eight, Bruce," said Mary.

"Old enough!"

"Santa's real, right, Mom?" asked Young Green, tears forming in his eyes.

"Of course he is, sweetie. I just don't know if he's coming this year."

Bruce hung his head slightly and shook it.

"Why wouldn't he come? I've been good all year, haven't I?" asked Young Green.

"He's not real, Noel," said Bruce. "I don't like seeing you get caught up in this stuff."

"Stop it, Bruce," said Mary. "Of course you've been good, Noel. You're always good."

"What about the watch I asked for? The one that talks and you can go underwater with?"

"You're not getting it!" said Bruce. "But how about *thanks for keeping the lights on, Pop*? I take complaints from people all day. My home is the one place I'd like a little appreciation. If you want a watch, get a job and buy one. You can't count on people to come through for you, especially not pretend people. Nothing in life is free."

"Stop!" shouted Mary.

"What are you going to tell him this year, Mary, when he runs in here and sees he didn't get anything he asked for? It's getting old; just tell him the truth."

"Maybe if you believed, or at least allowed him to believe, things would be different," cried Mary.

"Don't give him false hope!" yelled Bruce.

Young Green watched his parents through tears. He hated to see them fight; he would give up Christmas if it would make them stop.

Bruce got up and yanked Young Green's stocking off the mantle and threw it in the fire. "This ends now! I don't ever want to see another stocking in this house!"

Young Green ran out of the room, crying. He turned down the hall and went into his bedroom. He grabbed a letter that was sitting on his dresser, written in crayon. He could hear his parents arguing in the other room. Young Green looked at the letter.

Dear Santa Claus, this is Noel Green. I am 8 and have been real good this year. I don't want much, just the Secret Spy Series silver watch that can talk and go under the water. That is all. I am so excited, I can't wait until Christmas! Thank you, Noel Green. 3214 Cicero Street, Apartment 2D, Chicago, Illinois.

Young Green ripped the letter up into tiny pieces, opened his window, and threw it out. He crawled up onto his bed and covered his ears. Tears streamed down his cheeks.

Twenty-five years later, Green was asleep in a hospital bed. Winters, Veronica, and Santa were all waiting in the room.

"That's all I want," said Green, in a hazy dream state. Everybody in the room lit up with excitement.

"That's all I want . . . Veronica . . . ," Green trailed off.

Green was still unconscious. Santa and Winters looked at Veronica. She shrugged and shook her head as Green opened his eyes and tried to make out his surroundings.

"Ho, ho, ho. Atta' boy, Noelie!" said Santa.

"Sir?" Green was disoriented, but it all started to come back to him, the toy factory, and the explosion.

"Rise and shine, hero," said Winters.

"You saved Mr. Claus, Noel," said Veronica.

"Thank you, Green. You did a very brave thing," said Santa.

"Just doing my job," said Green, coming fully awake.

"Well, rest up, son. You deserve it," said Santa.

Green sat up. "Negative, sir, we need to find out who attacked us."

"You need to rest, get your strength back," said Veronica.

"Whoever did this isn't resting and you can bet your stuffed stockings they'll strike again." Green tried to get up, but winced at the pain in his shoulder.

Santa put a hand on his chest, easing him back down on the bed. "Rest, Agent Green. That's an order. Everything else can wait."

"Yes, sir," said Green, reluctant.

Santa nodded and left the room.

"Is there anything you need, buddy? Anything I can bring you?" asked Winters.

Green looked at his hospital gown. "My clothes. I've got to get out of here."

"But, Santa just said—"

"It's in Mr. Claus's best interest that I be on my feet right now."

"Okay, okay," said Winters before he took off out of the room.

Veronica looked at Green's bandaged shoulder. "Does it hurt?"

"I'm fine," Green said with a pained expression.

"How did you know a bomb was about to go off?" asked Veronica.

Green pointed to the back of his neck. "That guy in the elevator? He had a Southie tattoo on his neck."

"Southie? Like Boston?"

"No, Southie as in the South Pole. It's home to some nasty characters."

"You saved our lives, Noel." Veronica looked at Green, clearly impressed. "It would have taken out Santa and a good portion of his elves if it wasn't for you."

"They knew Mr. Claus was going to be doing a walk-through

yesterday. That's privileged information. They timed the explosion to go off exactly when Santa would have been in the building."

"Do you think it was somebody here?"

Green placed a reassuring hand on her arm. "I don't know yet, but I will find out. We need to keep a watchful eye."

Veronica leaned in closer toward Green. She placed her hand on his as they exchanged a look. "Yes, a watchful eye," she said, her gaze lingering over Green.

Winters burst through the door holding Green's suit and a handful of ties and Veronica backed away.

"Here you go, buddy! Man, you've got some ugly ties. I brought you a variety to choose from. I'd go with the black."

Green shot Winters an annoyed look.

"Am I interrupting something?" asked Winters.

Veronica ran her hand through her hair. "No, no, just thanking Green Agent, I mean Noel, here for his bravery and heroism. Okay, I'm gonna go. Bye." Veronica left in a hurry.

Winters turned to Green. "You salty dog!"

"What?" asked Green as he quickly slipped on his clothing.

"She's only got eyes for you," sang Winters.

"Oh, please, Winters. Can't you ever just focus on the job at hand?"

Winters held his hands up. "I'm just saying she's become an environmentalist."

Green paused, baffled. "What are you talking about?"

"She's *going Green!*"

Winters laughed as Green straightened his tie.

CHAPTER ELEVEN

Wood paneling lined the tall ceilings in Santa's office. Built-in shelves were filled with old books, first editions of many classics in literature, modern stories like the Harry Potter novels, and hundreds of encyclopedias, dictionaries, and atlases.

Many collectible toys and antiques adorned the room, including one of the original Steamboat Willie models and a baseball bat signed by Babe Ruth, Ted Williams, Jackie Robinson, and Willie Mays.

One wall was full of framed photographs of Santa posing with historically significant figures: Albert Einstein, Margaret Thatcher, Walt Disney, Martin Luther King, President Kennedy, Amelia Earhart, John Lennon, Nelson Mandela, Ronald Reagan, and many others.

Through a giant window was an expansive view of the North Pole Village. Santa leaned against a large, open fireplace and stared out the window, deep in thought as the orange glow from the fire illuminated his face.

Archer, the elf foreman, sat nearby as Santa continued to brood. Archer stood and walked over to Santa, sliding up next to him. "Sir, with this factory going down, I'm not certain we'll be able to finish everything before the big day."

Santa turned to face him. "We've faced trials before. We both know that we have the best staff in the world, and we still have our other factories. We'll be able to make up for the lost time if we work hard enough."

Green and Winters entered the room. "Sir, do you have a moment?" asked Green.

Santa turned and raised an eyebrow. "Noel, I thought I told you to stay in bed."

"I'm sorry, sir. This can't wait."

Santa left the fireplace and sat at his desk. Green dropped a folder containing a slew of photographs and documents on the surface.

"As you know, sir, we keep a file of potential threats to the North Pole," said Green. He slid two photographs of Frostbite out of the file. One photo was from surveillance footage taken before the bomb went off. The other was a black and white spy photo of Frostbite from a distance.

"This is the man that set off the bomb yesterday," said Winters. "His name is Frostbite."

"I've never seen him before," said Santa. Archer looked at the photo and shook his head.

Green slid out another photograph: a surveillance photo of Frostbite standing with Cole.

"We believe that Frostbite works for this elf," said Green.

Santa looked at the photo. "Cole."

"Who is Cole?" asked Winters.

"It's a long story," said Santa.

"Well, I think I'd better hear it," said Winters.

"Yes. Please sit down."

Green and Winters took a seat on a couch over by the window where Santa stood.

"As you know, this isn't the location of the original North Pole headquarters," said Santa.

"Yes, I've heard rumors of Pole One," said Winters.

"Long ago, before I came here, elves lived in and ran the North Pole."

Archer looked down.

"If this is too sensitive for you, you may leave, Archer," said Santa. Archer shook his head. "No, sir, I've made peace with the past."

"Very well," said Santa. "If you could imagine it, Pole One was even more grand than our current location. The village was larger and there was an enormous stone pillar that stood in the center of it, marking true North."

Winters sat forward. "Excuse me, but I don't know any of this, when it was, or how all of this started."

"That's another story," said Santa, dismissing Winters. "What you need to know is that back then, at Pole One, the elves had a king. He and I had an understanding and we lived in harmony. I was a little leaner back then, and I'm told I looked more like a wizard." Santa smiled at the memory. "Maybe I was too confident, too brazen, but I didn't place as high priority on security as we do now. But there was a . . . *force* that wanted to destroy Pole One. The Elf King and many elves joined this force and quite a few elves stayed loyal to me. One Christmas season this force attacked and we fled."

"I'm sorry, but what was this *force* that wanted to destroy Pole One?" asked Green.

Santa took a moment. "We don't need to dwell on that, it's long been over."

"I'm sorry, sir, but I think I need to know," said Winters.

Santa looked over all of them, debating what to tell them. "You do know, Noel, and I don't want to ever speak on it again."

Green sat back, a look of understanding on his face. "Krampus," he whispered.

Santa nodded once, his expression firm that there would be no more discussion. "And so we left Pole One and I banished all of the elves that followed Krampus, including the Elf King . . . who was Cole's great grandfather."

"That was a long time ago . . . ," said Archer.

"Eventually I created the SSS and recruited men who've been running security here ever since."

"We believe that Cole has someone on the inside, feeding him privileged information. He wants to hurt you. We need to put you in hiding, sir."

"Hiding? I don't like the idea of that so close to Christmas. We just lost our key toy factory, Agent Green. We're already behind!"

"That is exactly why it's so important that you go into hiding. Without you, there would be no Christmas," said Green. "The world almost lost you yesterday. It won't happen again, not on my watch."

"Maybe you're right," said Santa.

"There's one more thing, sir. If Cole does have someone on the inside, the disclosure of your hiding place must not leave this room."

"And exactly where am I going, Agent Green?" asked Santa.

"The last place anybody would expect to find you."

CHAPTER TWELVE

A black Suburban was parked in front of an old apartment building on a street in New York City. Men walking up and down the street wore the long beards and *payos* indicative of Hasidic Judaism.

Inside the Suburban, Winters sat in the drivers seat, and Green sat shotgun. In the back were Santa and Mrs. Claus, dressed in traditional Hasidic Jewish attire. They look convincing as an old Jewish couple, especially Santa with his long beard.

"Are you sure about this, Agent Green?" asked Santa.

"Absolutely. These are good people, and they don't celebrate Christmas. Nobody would expect you to be here."

Winters and Green got out, checking with other unseen agents that the coast was clear. They led Santa and Mrs. Claus inside a humble apartment.

"I know it's not much to look at, but it is temporary, sir," said Green. "Just until we can guarantee your safety back at the Pole."

"Oh, don't worry about us, Noelie, we'll be just fine, won't we Santa?" asked Mrs. Claus.

Santa looked around. "If you think this is the safest place for us to be, we'll make it work."

"Thank you, Santa, or I should say Mr. Clausenstein. You'll be safe here," said Green.

"I've never heard New York City being referred to as safe," said Winters.

"Don't worry about us. Go find Cole and stop him," said Santa.

CHAPTER THIRTEEN

Cole was practicing his golf stroke with black golf balls and a tiny putter as Frostbite entered the room.

"Sit down, Frostbite" said Cole.

Frostbite obliged. "Sir, I did everything—"

"Shut up! Don't say one more word, you despicable freak! Do you want to explain to me why that over-stuffed jolly fool is still alive?"

"I—"

"Silence!" Cole hurled his putter against the wall. Frostbite sat silently, not sure if he should speak or not.

"Speak, you imbecile," ordered Cole.

"Somehow Green knew, sir."

"Somehow? It's because you were sloppy."

"That's not all, sir. Black is reporting that they've got Claus in hiding."

Cole sighed. "Where?"

"He didn't know, sir. It's classified," said Frostbite.

"All right, Green. You wanna play? I'll play your reindeer games."

"Uh, good?" asked Frostbite.

"Of course it's good!" Cole got up and walked over to a large map of the North Pole. "I'll just have to improvise." Cole thought for a moment and he knew exactly how he could still pull off his Plan B. "Of course!"

"What is it, sir?" asked Frostbite.

Cole grabbed a glass of rotten milk off of his desk. "Need to know, Frosty. Need to know."

"Do I need to know?"

"No, you do not. That's the entire reason that phrase exists. You don't tell someone something is 'need to know' and then tell them what it is. I am surrounded by dullards!"

"Yes, sir." Frostbite turned and left.

Cole took a long drink of his sour milk, leaving a thick, chunky mustache on his upper lip. He sank back in his chair, clicking his unkempt nails together, a knowing smile creeping across his face.

CHAPTER FOURTEEN

Agent Black and Veronica sat across from each other in a booth inside the Northern Lights Tavern.

"Thanks for rescuing me from another endless night of paperwork. I needed a break," said Veronica.

Black nodded. "What's the latest on the Macy's Thanksgiving Day Parade? Is that still on?"

"It is as far as I know. That is the event that single-handedly launches the Christmas season. Children expect to see him there."

"So, Green and Winters should be getting back soon. Any idea where they went?" asked Black.

"I don't know, Agent Black. They didn't tell me. It's classified, I guess."

"Yeah, they didn't tell me either, and I'm SSS, for Pete's sake!"

"I guess they feel they can't be cautious enough at this point, with a spy lurking among us and all."

"Does Green have any idea who it is?"

"Not that I know of," said Veronica.

Black checked his watch. "It's getting late. May I escort you home?"

"That's very kind of you, Agent Black."

Black smiled.

Veronica's cottage was cozy and tastefully decorated with a plush red couch with silver snowflake–embroidered pillows and vintage Christmas posters from *Life* magazine covers. She opened the front door and turned to face Black on the front porch.

"Thanks for walking me home, Agent Black—I mean, Arnold. It was very sweet of you."

"It was my pleasure," said Black.

"Good night."

"Good night, Veronica."

Veronica closed the door and turned on a lamp.

Outside, Black backed away from Veronica's cottage slowly, looking around in the dark. He checked his watch and slinked into the shadows.

The double doors of the hangar garage where Santa's sleigh was stored and maintained were opened wide. Cody and a couple of mechanics stood by as Santa's sleigh came into view in the sky.

A hangar security guard guided the sleigh in with glowing red and green batons.

Rudolph led the A-team as they touched down, returning from New York City. Green and Winters stepped out of the sleigh as Cody unhooked the reindeer team.

"Welcome back, sir," said Cody.

"Thank you, Cody," said Green. "The sleigh is in great condition and the reindeer seem to be in top shape."

"We'll keep things up and running until Mr. and Mrs. Claus can return," said Cody.

"That's right, Cody. For all of us here it's business as usual," said Winters.

"Well, not quite usual," said Cody.

"No. Winters and I will be handling most of Santa's duties. But we must keep Christmas preparation on schedule. We're keeping a sharp eye out, Cody, but the Pole is secure."

Green and Winters made their way to the back of the hangar. Two SSS agents stood guard by the doors.

* * *

Back in her cottage, Veronica set a kettle on the stove. She pressed PLAY on her answering machine. *Hello Veronica, this is Agent Noel Green, I mean Noel. I tried you at your office, but you weren't there. I just wanted to let you know that Mr. Claus is safe. Talk to you later. This is Agent Noel Green, by the way.*

Veronica smiled at Green's awkwardness.

* * *

Green and Winters walked away from the hangar.

"Let's go find Veronica and give her an update on Mr. and Mrs. Claus," said Green.

"You go find Veronica yourself; I'll be in the tavern," said Winters.

"This isn't a social engagement, Winters. This is work-related."

Winters rolled his eyes. "Oh yes, sir. Absolutely, sir."

Green shook his head and led Winters toward Veronica's cottage.

Veronica finished hanging mistletoe in the hall, humming "Baby It's Cold Outside." She grabbed a cup of cocoa from the kitchen and snagged a copy of *The Christmas Box* off the coffee table as she headed into her bedroom.

A large shadow in the darkened living room moved across one of the moonlit windows. The floor creaked, stopping Veronica in her tracks. "Hello . . . ?"

Nothing. She stepped in a wet puddle and noticed several over-sized, half-melted, snowy footprints on the carpet. Her gaze followed the footprints to a dark corner where the shadow moved again, followed by a low growl.

Veronica rushed for the door and the shadow moved into the light, revealing the white beast Avalanche.

Green and Winters made their way down a snowy path toward Veronica's cottage.

"So, if we're watching a movie and I just put my hand down close to hers, she'll reach over and hold it?" asked Green.

"Just how long has it been since you've been on a date with an actual girl?" laughed Winters.

Veronica's screams cut through the quiet night air.

Green sprinted toward Veronica's cottage, pulling his Freeze Ray out of its holster, Winters right behind him.

They flew across a pristine snowfield, never slowing as they approached the cottage. Green burst through the door.

"Veronica!" Green shouted, as Winters came in behind him. They scanned the cottage; overturned lamps and furniture showed signs of a struggle. The contents of Veronica's broken cocoa mug were spilled across the floor.

Green headed to her bedroom as Winters turned for the kitchen. The back door to the kitchen was wide open.

"Green! Out the back!" yelled Winters.

Green and Winters raced out the back door.

Agent Black slinked from the shadows, watching them flee into the night. He turned and ran in the opposite direction.

Green and Winters streaked across the frozen snow. Veronica screamed again. This time it was distant, out across the icy tundra.

"Whatever grabbed her is moving fast!" shouted Green. Green spoke into his candy cane pin. "All agents! This is Green. Winters and I are in pursuit of an intruder who has taken Miss Snow. We need backup; this is an emergency!"

Green looked down and saw Avalanche's large footprints in the snow. He and Winters sprinted, following the trail.

Black stood by Santa's hangar, hidden from the view of two agents standing guard. He heard Green's message over his SSS communications earpieces and waited until the agents ran off into the night to give Green backup.

Black walked through the hangar carrying an attaché case. Santa's sleigh, minus the reindeer, was suspended on a lift.

Biff and Cliff, human mechanics, worked on different parts of

Santa's sleigh, as it was hooked up to a diagnostics computer. Biff and Cliff were brothers who had worked for NASA before Santa discovered their talents and recruited them to work at the North Pole. They loved tinkering with science and the touch of magic that was available to them at the Pole, though Santa was always reminding them not to try tinkering too much. There were boundaries and Santa made sure they stayed within them.

"Evening, boys," said Black.

"Hello, sir. What can we do for you?" asked Cliff.

"I'm afraid I'm going to have to ask you gentlemen to take five. I've been given orders to search these premises for any lethal devices."

"Of course, no problem. We could use a break anyway," said Biff.

Cliff and Biff left and Black got to work inspecting the sleigh, opening compartments and pressing switches.

As Green and Winters crested a snowy ridge, they saw Avalanche toss Veronica into Cole's sleigh. Cole's sleigh looked nothing like Santa's, except for the fact that it had a car's body for its carriage.

Cole had chosen a 1962 Lincoln Continental with the front-opening rear doors hinged at the rear, the so-called "suicide doors" no longer seen on modern vehicles.

Cole's sleigh was sleek black with white runners, Cole's homage to the whitewall tires popular on the vehicle in the 60s. Stationed at the front was a ferocious wolf team.

"Veronica!" yelled Green.

The wolves turned and snarled at Green and Winters.

Cole cracked the reins and the wolf team jolted into action, pulling the sleigh across the snow and into the air.

Green and Winters chased behind the sleigh. Winters pulled out his Freeze Ray but Green held his hand down.

"Don't!" yelled Green.

Cole's sleigh pulled high into the sky and disappeared as Veronica's screams faded in the night air.

Green fell to his knees, panting.

"What was that?" asked Winters.

"It looked like the abominable snowman . . . in a sleigh . . . pulled by flying dogs," said Green.

"What the heck is going on here?" cried Winters.

Agent Burke's voice was transmitted through Green's candy cane pin. "Agent Green, sir. This is Burke. The lead mechanics of Santa's sleigh just called us. Over."

"I read you, Burke, loud and clear. Over," said Green.

"We have a serious problem, sir. Over."

Green and Winters looked at each other. *What now?*

Green and Winters bolted into the hangar. Cliff and Biff were waiting for them.

"One of your agents took Mr. Claus's Time Expander, sir," said Cliff.

"That's impossible," said Green.

"We were doing routine diagnostics on the Time Expander, when in comes one of your agents, name of Black, I believe," said Cliff. "He tells us he's got orders to inspect the sleigh and me and Cliff should go and take a break. So we did. We got donuts and coffee like we are known to do. When we get back, I turn on the diagnostics machine, only to find the Time Expander ain't working!"

"Black. I never liked that guy," said Winters.

"Let him finish," said Green.

"Right. So I took a look at it; and what do ya know? Somebody switched it out and put in a dummy one."

Biff pointed at a fake piece of machinery inside the inner workings of the sleigh.

"It looks like it comprises used pinball machine parts," said Winters.

Green spoke into his pin. "Agent Black! Come in, Agent Black. Do you copy?"

There was a pause and then soft laughter came back over Green's pin.

Green yelled into the pin. "Who is this?"

Cole's voice came back over the pin. "Well, if it isn't the heroic Agent Noel Green I've heard so much about."

"Cole," said Green.

"I like to think of myself as the Anti-Claus, but, sure, you can call me Cole. That's another of my many names."

"What do you want, Cole? You've already got the Time Expander."

"Santa Claus! I want to know where you're hiding the fat man," said Cole, over the pin.

"Nothing you could do would make me tell you," said Green.

"Nothing, you say? What about your little girlie, Miss Snow? What if I sent her back to you as a precious ice sculpture?"

"I promise you, Cole. You're not going to get away with this."

"Blah, blah, blah. Whatever you say, Greenie. Just stop with the hero talk and give me what I want. There is no sense in protecting that fat gift lover. You have one day. Otherwise, I swear to silver bells, I'm going to freeze Miss Snow here."

"Now listen, you—" The transmission died.

"What are we going to do?" asked Winters.

"The only thing we can do," said Green. Green turned to Cliff. "Is the GPS system on the Time Expander functioning?"

Cliff tapped a few keys on a computer screen inside Santa's sleigh. A flashing red GPS dot on a map popped up. "Yes, sir. But you can only track it on here."

"Get the sleigh ready!" shouted Green as he ran out, Winters on his heels.

CHAPTER FIFTEEN

Green and Winters rushed into the stables wrapped in warm, hooded coats. Cody was attending to the reindeer.

"What can I do for you gents?" asked Cody.

"I need you to get Tinsel and the B-team ready for flight, Cody." said Green.

"Sir?"

"We have an emergency, we need to be in the air ASAP," replied Winters.

"Uh, yes, sirs! Right away! You don't want Rudolph?"

"Not tonight. Let the A-Team rest up; they've had a long ride today. Tinsel is my boy," said Green. "Get them to Santa's hangar!"

Back at the hangar, one of Cody's stable hands finished harnessing the reindeer to the sleigh. Cliff and Biff were doing some last minute mechanical work. Winters and Green stood by.

Cody entered the hangar with Tinsel. "The fog is very thick tonight, Agent Green."

"Yes, I see that."

"Tinsel's got one of the brightest noses I ever seen," said Cody.

"He'll do just fine," said Green, knowing Cody had a special place in his heart for Tinsel.

"I swear by this reindeer. He's stout and he's brave. He'll guide you true."

Green nodded and Cody harnessed Tinsel to the head of the team.

As Cliff and Biff finished their testing, Cliff pulled Green aside. "Looks like you're heading to the South Pole."

"Yes."

"Lotta ice down there, I'd imagine," said Cliff.

"Yes, Cliff, there is a quite a bit of ice, I'm sure."

Cliff looked around, making sure no one was watching. He handed Green a metallic device in the shape of a candy cane.

"What's this?"

"If you need to break down any ice structures, just fix that to the ice and stand back," said Cliff, a gleam in his eye.

"Cliff, is this within SSS protocols?"

"Oh yes, sir, I promise."

Green shook hands with Cliff and got in the cabin of Santa's sleigh next to Winters. He hit a series of switches and went through a quick pre-flight checklist. Winters double checked the gauges and nodded to Green.

Cliff and Biff gave Winters and Green thumbs up as Green took the reins. "Yaw! On, Tinsel! Onward, boys!"

The reindeer levitated as the hangar doors opened and Green flew the sleigh out into the stormy night. Gaining speed, the sleigh flew high into the air. The green light from Tinsel's nose cut through the thick, stormy clouds.

Cole stood with Frostbite and Ivy on a grand balcony overlooking a vast space full of creepy ice statues; some were hideous-looking beasts, some wolves, and many, many penguins.

"I've always felt most at home in my mausoleum," said Cole.

"This place gives me the creeps," said Ivy.

"Ah, you're kind to say that."

Black entered followed by Avalanche, who carried Veronica. Veronica's hands were tied and her mouth gagged.

"Everybody, we have a very special guest with us tonight!" said Cole. "Welcome to my humble abode, Miss Snow."

Veronica looked around with fearful eyes at the frightening statues.

"Yes, please look around and get a taste of what your fate will be if your boyfriend doesn't disclose Santa's location."

The others, except for Avalanche and Ivy, laughed.

"They are impressive, aren't they?" asked Cole. "You might think a master craftsman carved them, but alas, such is not the case."

Cole slid down a curved chute to the ice floor beneath the balcony while the others took the icy stairs. He glided over to an ice cage where several penguins were kept. Opening the cage, he took out one of the cute animals.

"Come here, little fella. Let Uncle Cole hold you."

The penguin seemed happy to be held. "You may not realize it, but the penguin is a filthy, disgusting animal. All of those movies about being cute and dancing are a lie! You've never seen so much guano!"

Frostbite scrunched his nose. "What's guano?"

"Guano! Their scat, their dung. Must I always be educating you, Frosty?"

"I don't know technical terms for penguin leavings, sorry, sir."

Cole rolled his eyes; he wasn't going to let Frostbite's ignorance throw off his little show. He walked over to a chamber the size of a phone booth and opened it, placing the penguin inside. He pressed a few buttons on a panel next to the chamber.

"Did you know that the bodies of most living beings are made up of over 60 percent water?" asked Cole. "Remarkable, isn't it?"

The chamber emitted an intense blue light, and a high-pitched beeping pierced the air. They all covered their ears and shut their eyes as the chamber filled with a blue mist. When it stopped, Cole opened the door, reached in and slid the penguin out. It was now solid ice!

Avalanche moaned, saddened by the sight. Veronica gasped.

"You see! I'll give that sorry sap Green one day to tell me where that stuffed turkey Claus is, or I'm sticking you in there," Cole said to Veronica. "A woman of your beauty would make a delightful addition to my collection. You better hope your boyfriend comes through."

Veronica's words came out muffled through her restraint. Cole stepped over to her and removed her gag.

"Yes, my dear?"

"He's not my boyfriend," said Veronica.

CHAPTER SIXTEEN

A red light flashed on the GPS screen mounted in the dash of Santa's sleigh, marking the Time Expander's location. Agent Green drove the sleigh across the desolate snow-white tundra of the South Pole.

"We're getting close," Green said to Winters.

The sleigh bells on the reindeer harnesses jingled loudly.

"These bells are going to ruin the element of surprise . . . we'll have to park a ways out and hike in," said Green.

"Yeah, this isn't exactly a stealth vehicle," said Winters. "You can't sneak up on the bad guys in the jolly-mobile."

The red dot on the GPS display began to blink rapidly, signifying that they were very close to the Time Expander. Green guided the sleigh closer to the ground. He searched the area and found a stretch of flat terrain suitable for landing.

In the distance the tall, spear-like spires of Cole's Ice Palace loomed ominously.

In yet another room in Cole's expansive lair was a setup patterned after war rooms in classic movies. One wall was comprised of massive display screens, showing intricate layouts of the North and South Poles and all of the continents. The walls were icy blue, draped with transparent screens that displayed data and imagery from satellites aimed directly at the North Pole and security camera feeds on the streets of New York City.

On another end of the room an enormous portrait of Cole looking stoic, hung on the wall. A portrait of Napoleon, Cole's hero, in the exact pose, hung next to it.

An outsized table with a surface displaying a backlit map of the world, stood at the center of the room. Cole told people that it was for strategy planning, but in reality he just thought it looked cool. Like most things in Cole's fortress, vanity was the primary motivator.

The map on the table was peppered with intricately carved models; there was Cole and Santa, Green and Winters, Frostbite and Ivy, as well as Santa's sleigh, Cole's Ice Palace, and the North Pole.

Cole led Veronica over to the table. She was no longer bound, but Frostbite stood sentry by the door.

"Can I interest you in a glass of warm rancid milk, sweetheart?" asked Cole.

"You're disgusting," said Veronica.

"Any more talk like that and you're likely to be put on the naughty list. Oh wait, how silly of me. That ridiculous tradition will soon be history!"

"That's what all of this is about? You want to destroy Christmas?"

Cole spewed out a mouthful of rancid milk. "Are you mad? Why would anyone want to do that? I don't want to destroy Christmas; I want to save Christmas!"

"By killing Santa and blowing up a toy factory?" asked Veronica.

"All great change is preceded by chaos. It's all part of the greater good. I will restore Christmas to its rightful place."

"But Christmas is Santa."

"No it isn't," said Cole.

Cole looked around at the scope of his war room and strutted proudly. "It's taken me years to put this all together. Countless days of toiling and working to weave the threads of genius together and amass this grand Christmas revolution you're about to witness. I'll soon be known as the revolutionary who took Christmas into the 21st century by taking it back to its origins!"

Veronica looked around the war room, overwhelmed by the scope of Cole's plan. She had no idea what exactly Cole was plotting, just that he was filled with hate. "Why, Cole? Why do you hate Santa Claus so much?"

Cole's cool exterior finally cracked. He picked up the model of Santa and smashed it down, shattering the glass map. His hand bled from the broken glass. He pointed a bloody finger at Veronica and looked her dead in the eyes.

"WHO DOES HE THINK HE IS?" Cole's voice echoed loudly throughout the cavernous war room. Cole's smirk was gone, and as he turned to Veronica, his scowl tightened and his eyes bore down on her. Veronica was visibly shaken as she backed away from Cole's alarming show of hostility.

"He judges and condemns! Nice list. Naughty list. Who is he to judge? Who gave him the authority to start making lists, and to force his agenda on children? Who appointed him Lord of the North Pole? Elves were there long before Santa showed up! My father—" Cole gathered himself and pointed at Veronica. "Did you vote for Santa Claus?"

Veronica stepped away from Cole. At that moment Cole was not a tiny elf; he was a titan of hate. Cole saw her fear and it gave him pause. He took a breath, composing himself.

"Well, I didn't vote for Santa Claus. Seems to me, like any other dictator . . . he appointed himself." Cole looked at his bloody hand and walked over to the shattered map. "And like any other dictator, he can be overthrown."

Cole's attention was diverted by a flashing red light, which appeared on several of the room's large screens.

"Well, my dear, I have matters to attend to." Cole turned to Frostbite. "Escort our guest to her quarters."

Frostbite placed freezing ice-like shackles on Veronica's wrists and escorted her out of the room.

Cole reached down to the cracked map with his finger and drew a bloody X over New York City.

Green and Winters had reached Cole's massive ice fortress and were crouched down, hiding behind a snowdrift.

"I'm willing to bet the star off the top of your Christmas tree that they'll be waiting for us in there," said Green.

"How do you suggest we get inside?" asked Winters.

Green reached into his jacket pocket and pulled out the candy cane device that Cliff had given him. "Follow me."

Green snuck up to the large ice wall on the east side of the palace. He pressed the candy cane device to the side of the ice wall and took three large steps back.

Winters raised an eyebrow at Green as he also took three large steps back.

They stood there in silence, looking at the metallic device. It started glowing bright green. All of a sudden lines of green shot from the top and the bottom of the candy cane, moving out and away from the device, zigzagging all across the ice wall, until they met, forming the shape of a Christmas tree.

Winters raised an eyebrow. "Well, that's pretty, Green, but how does it help us?"

Green shrugged as the green lines turned a bright red and the lines began moving in, back toward the device, melting the shape out of the ice.

Green and Winters stared as the candy cane device dropped to the ground and a giant hole in the shape of a Christmas tree was left.

"Well, I guess that's one of the disadvantages of a giant ice palace. It melts," said Green.

"Wow! Where did you get that thingy?" asked Winters.

"Shhh! Let's go."

Winters trudged ahead as Green reached down and snatched up the candy cane device. "Cliff, you sly fox," he said to himself.

In Cole's kennel, Frostbite removed Veronica's shackles and stuck her in a cage across from Avalanche. Frostbite smiled at her and then left.

Veronica grabbed the bars of her cage. "I'm not scared of you Southies or this snow ape!"

The yelling startled Avalanche. He huddled into one of the cage's corners.

Veronica looked Avalanche over. "You're more afraid of me than I am of you." She walked close to her bars and examined his. "You're a prisoner. You're just like me, aren't you?"

Avalanche raised his eyebrows.

"What's your name?"

Avalanche did not reply.

"Do you have a name? Can you speak?"

Avalanche pointed to himself and answered in a deep voice. "A - fa - lanch!"

Veronica laughed. "Avalanche? Is that right, your name is Avalanche? My name is Ver - on - i - ca," she said slowly.

"Fur - on - ka," said Avalanche.

Veronica nodded. "Yes, that's close enough." She sat down. "You gave me quite a scare back at the North Pole."

Avalanche looked down in shame.

"Well, I won't hold it against you."

Avalanche pointed toward Veronica. "Out?" he said.

"Yes, Avalanche, out. I would love to get out. How do we get out of here?"

Avalanche retreated into the shadows of his cage. "Me no go."

"Cole's got you terrified. But you don't need to be afraid of him. My friends are coming, Avalanche."

"Fur - end?"

"Yes, don't you have friends?"

Avalanche looked down, shaking his head.

"Friends are the people, or not always people I guess, who care about us. The people I work with are coming. Noel's coming. We can help you. I promise you won't be hurt. I won't let Cole lay a hand on you."

Avalanche looked up tentatively.

"I need your help. I can't get out of here without you," said Veronica. "Besides, an amazing creature like you should never be kept in a cage. You deserve to be free. He can't get away with this! It makes me sick!" Veronica's eyes were ablaze with fury. "I know he forced you to kidnap me, but you were very gentle with me when you took me away from my home."

Avalanche lowered his head again in shame.

"Avalanche, no! I'm not mad at you! It wasn't your fault. But you don't need to follow Cole anymore. He doesn't own you. You are much stronger than he is. Please help me."

Veronica extended her thin arm outside her cage and reached toward Avalanche. He could only manage to get his thick fingers through the bars. Veronica grabbed his massive thumb.

Avalanche looked down at their hands, then up at Veronica. "Fur end?"

"Yes," replied Veronica. "We are."

Avalanche stood forward, his chest puffed out, his confidence growing.

"That's right, Avalanche, I am your friend! You can do this!"

"Mee hep you!" Avalanche grasped the bars and pulled with all his strength, slowly bending the metal bars back.

Green and Winters crept their way into Cole's gaudy mausoleum filled with the frozen ice sculptures.

"Wow. This place is creepy," whispered Winters.

"Shhh! Do you want to get us caught?" asked Green.

"Sorry." Winters didn't see the small ice penguin on the floor as he bumped into it. The shatter echoed through the frigid halls. Both men froze.

"You always were a second-rate agent, Winters," a dark figure said, emerging from the archway at the back of the mausoleum.

Green and Winters drew their Freeze Rays, pointing them toward the voice.

"Black," said Green.

"You two-faced traitor!" yelled Winters. "I always knew something was off about you."

Black whipped out his Blast Ray, a destructive gift from Cole.

"Where's Veronica?" asked Green.

"She seems pretty comfortable here, Green. Face it, you're not getting what you want for Christmas this year."

Black raised his weapon and pointed it at Green but before he could shoot, Green fired his Freeze Ray at Black. A bolt of green lightning zapped across the room in Black's direction.

Black dove behind a statue just in time and fired back. A large bolt of red lightning shot across the room. Green and Winters jumped out of the way just as the red bolt hit an ice statue of a polar bear and blew it to pieces.

They exchanged Freeze and Blast Ray fire, cracking up and melting the surrounding statues.

Veronica and Avalanche heard the commotion as they moved down a long corridor. Red and green flashes illuminated the ice castle.

Veronica peered around the corner and her heart leapt when she saw that Green had come to her rescue.

One of Black's red bolts hit the penguin cage, busting a large hole in the side. Penguins scattered as they fled out of the cage.

Black spun at a sound behind him. He faced a wall of white fur. Avalanche grabbed Black by the collar and lifted him off the ground.

Green and Winters watched as the beast held the kicking and screaming Black in the air.

"That's the monster that took Veronica!" shouted Winters.

Green took aim, Avalanche and Black in his sights when Veronica leapt out of her hiding place, shielding Avalanche from Green's aim. "Noel!"

"Veronica!" Green lowered his weapon and sprinted toward Veronica as two dark figures appeared down the corridor behind her: Cole and Frostbite. "Watch out!" yelled Green.

Frostbite snatched Veronica as she screamed. Avalanche turned toward Veronica and roared.

Cole grabbed a sharp sliver of ice from one of the broken statues and held it to Veronica's throat. "Everybody stop or the girl gets it!" shouted Cole. Cole looked around the room at the shattered ice sculptures; penguins wandered everywhere.

"You've made quite a mess of my private collection, Agent Green. Now drop your weapons before I redecorate the room with Miss Snow here."

"Let her go, Cole," said Winters.

"Just tell me where you're hiding Santa Claus and I'll gladly see you all safely home."

"Don't tell him!" Veronica said. "He has the Time Expander and is going to kill—" Frostbite covered her mouth before she could finish.

"Thank you for stating the obvious, dear. Agent Green, it's no secret I want to kill the Claus, but there doesn't seem to be a thing you can do about it! I have the Time Expander and your girl. Now tell me where he is!"

As Cole stood there threatening them, Green looked calmly back at him. "Cole, I will give you one chance to make a deal to save yourself. Hand over Miss Snow and the Time Expander and I will see to it that you're taken out of here alive."

"You're a fool, Green. I'll never let her go and you'll never find the Time Expander. It's tucked away far from here. You're out of options."

Green pulled out a small device with an antenna and a green button.

"What is that?" asked Cole, his eyes darting.

"A detonator."

"For what?"

"The Time Expander."

Winters and Veronica looked just as surprised as Cole.

"You wouldn't destroy the Time Expander," said Cole, forcing a laugh. "That tub of lard couldn't do anything without it."

"You think with a device as important as that, we'd only have one?" asked Green. "Do you really think that this *exact* scenario had never occurred to Santa?"

"Ha! You're bluffing, Green Bean! If you could destroy it so easily, you would have done it already!"

"You see, Cole, your evil twisted mind could never consider the lives and well being of others so you'd never understand this, but I had to be sure that Miss Snow wasn't anywhere near the Time Expander when I detonated it."

Green smiled and pressed the button. A deep concussion from an explosion somewhere in the ice palace shook the ground. A resonate crunch echoed through the chamber as a massive crack erupted through the wall of the mausoleum.

Fire and ice exploded through the corridor, throwing Cole, Frostbite, and Veronica to the ground. Avalanche dropped Black.

Stalactites of ice broke free from the ceiling, crashing on the ground close to Green and Winters.

Frostbite scrambled to his feet and picked up Cole to shield him from the stalactites.

"Get your pasty mitts off of me!" Frostbite dropped Cole, who looked at Green. "This isn't over!"

Cole scurried into the corridor followed by Frostbite and Black.

Hurdling fallen ice statues and penguins out of his way, Winters rushed into the corridor after Cole.

Green dashed toward Veronica, who was already on her feet.

"Don't worry, I'm fine! Cole's getting away," said Veronica.

"I need to get you out. This place is coming down!" yelled Green.

Veronica pointed at Avalanche. "He's with me. Go; I'll be fine."

"Him?" asked Green. "Didn't he—"

"Noel, go now!"

"I'm not leaving you."

Veronica put a hand on Green's arm and looked him in the eye. "I'm fine. Go get him, Noel."

Green nodded and darted after Winters into the corridor as

another massive crack appeared along the ground. Avalanche tried to shepherd penguins out toward the exit.

"Avalanche! We have to get out of here!" said Veronica. "Do you know the way?"

Avalanche nodded. She took him by the hand, trying to lead him out of the room, but he pulled back, pointing to the penguins. "Tuk - see - dohs!"

Avalanche shooed the penguins toward the exit with his massive hands. Veronica looked at the cracks forming in the ceiling above them, and then quickly helped Avalanche herd the penguins to safety.

Cole and Frostbite bolted down the icy corridor as Black exchanged fire with Green and Winters, who weren't far behind. The ground shook and debris fell from the ceiling.

Ivy stepped out of her room. "Cole, what's happening?"

"Come, my dear. We're leaving," said Cole. He grabbed Ivy and pulled her down the corridor.

"But I need to grab my things."

"There's no time."

"I'm not leaving without my things!"

"Frostbite," Cole gestured and Frostbite lifted Ivy in the air and carried her along.

"Hey! Let go of me, you big oaf!" yelled Ivy.

Back down the corridor, Green and Winters were pinned down as they exchanged fire with Black.

"We don't have time for this," said Green.

Black fired his Blast Ray into the ceiling, tearing a hole through it as falling debris blocked the passage between them.

"Let's get out of here!" yelled Winters.

Cole, Frostbite, and Ivy climbed aboard Cole's sleigh. The wolf team was all hooked up and ready to go. Ice, like supersonic hail, fell from the ceiling all around them inside Cole's hangar.

Cole grabbed the reins.

"What about Black?" asked Ivy.

Cole glanced over his shoulder and then back at Ivy. "He's no longer of any use to me."

Cole cracked the reins and the wolf team pulled the sleigh out of the hanger and into the sky as Black ran outside.

"Cole! Wait, you forgot me!" yelled Black.

One side of Cole's Ice Palace collapsed as rapidly spreading cracks formed all over the exterior.

The massive doors to the main entrance broke free. Penguins poured from the doorway. Veronica, Green, and Winters ran through the door amidst the penguins with Avalanche close behind, his arms full of yet more penguins. Snowy dust billowed out in clouds behind them as the palace imploded.

Green watched Avalanche place the penguins on the ground; the white beast looked at Green with a big smile.

"Tuk - see - doh!"

Green turned to Veronica, still trying to catch his breath. "Veronica. How? What is this thing?"

"I'll explain later. Let's get out of here," said Veronica. "How'd you get here?"

"This way!" Green led Veronica, Winters, and Avalanche across the snowfield to Santa's sleigh.

"Buckle up, everyone," said Green. He tugged the reins and the reindeer levitated, lifting the sleigh into the air.

CHAPTER SEVENTEEN

Santa's sleigh roared through the sky with Winters now at the reins. Avalanche rested in the back row. Veronica turned to Green with gratitude in her eyes.

"I didn't think I was going to ever leave the South Pole alive."

"I'm glad we came when we did," said Green.

"What do you think Cole will do now?"

"He'll keep trying to destroy Santa and steal the Time Expander."

"I can't believe he thinks he can take over Christmas."

"He's out of control and egomaniacal. People like Cole can't imagine that their anger isn't justified."

"Well, I'm glad you got me out of there. You guys risked your lives to save me. I'll never forget that."

"You're worth the risk. Besides, I'm getting pretty good at saving your life, Miss Snow. The first two are on the house, but I'm afraid I'll have to charge you for any future rescues."

Veronica slid her hand over and clutched Green's.

"Thank you, Noel," she said. She rested her head on his shoulder. Green hesitated at first, but then slowly put his arm around her.

Winters watched the two in the rearview mirror. "Oh, brother," he said to himself.

Inside a very different sleigh pulled by very different animals, Cole cracked the reins of his wolf team with Ivy at his side. Frostbite lounged in the back seat.

"Where are we going, Cole?" asked Ivy.

"North," said Cole. "New York City."

"Why are we going there?" asked Frostbite.

"Because, albino-breath, tomorrow's Thanksgiving and I know where that chubby, stocking stuffer will be."

"But I didn't get to pack anything," said Ivy.

"Well, not to worry, my dear. I'll just have to get you a whole new wardrobe when we arrive."

Ivy clapped her hands. "Oh goody, shopping!"

Ivy hugged Cole. Cole bristled at the affection, his total focus on his plan to bring down Santa Claus.

Inside a community center in New York City, a group, along with Santa and Mrs. Claus, danced to traditional Jewish folk music. Santa and Mrs. Claus enjoyed themselves. He pulled her close to him and gave her a small kiss on the cheek. She giggled as he gently twirled her. He had surprisingly graceful moves and had always been able to sweep Mrs. Claus off her feet.

"After all these years, you still dance very well, my bubeleh," said Santa.

Mrs. Claus blushed. "Not too bad yourself, tubby," she teased.

"What a wonderful culture. So much dancing!" Santa spun away from Mrs. Claus and danced to his own beat, the crowd clapping and encouraging him. Santa swooped Mrs. Claus back into his arms, bending her at the waist. He kissed her before lifting her back up. "It's gonna be a shame to have to leave this place."

A beeping noise came from Santa's Apple Watch, startling them. "Which may be happening now. Come, my dear, we need to get back to the apartment."

Santa and Mrs. Claus danced their way to the door, making their way out of the community center and on to the street. They walked a few blocks to their apartment.

Inside, Santa pressed a few buttons on their stereo, while Mrs. Claus rushed to the window and closed the curtains. A built-in bookshelf slid back into the wall, revealing a large screen. Green appeared, speaking to them from inside the sleigh via an in-dash camera.

"Hello, Agent Green," said Mrs. Claus.

"Sir. Ma'am," Green replied.

"I hope you have good news for me, Noel," said Santa.

"Are you all right, sir? Has anybody spotted you?"

"No, nobody," said Santa.

"Good! We're on our way to you right now."

"Travel safe; we'll see you soon." Santa hit a switch and the screen hid away. He turned and looked out the window. Mrs. Claus went to him and put a comforting hand on his shoulder.

Back on Santa's sleigh, Green hit a button and a screen on the dash flipped closed. He spoke into his candy cane pin. "Come in, North Pole. This is Agent Green. Over."

Agent Burke's voice came back, "We read you, Agent Green. Over."

"All agents are to report for parade duty tomorrow in New York City. Cole is still at large. Over."

"Copy that, Agent Green. All agents will report for duty at the Macy's Thanksgiving Day Parade. Over."

"That's an affirmative, North Pole. Over and out."

Green leaned back by Veronica as they passed in front of a large, bright moon. Stars twinkled in the night sky as the sleigh neared the ocean. Ahead, the moon's reflection on the water painted a silver pathway along the shore.

"Doesn't it bring out the kid in you?" asked Veronica.

Green pondered the question. "No," he said.

"Are you kidding? We work for Santa Claus and we're flying in his sleigh!"

"Feeling like a kid at Christmas is not a place I like to revisit," said Green.

"Why would you say that, Noel?"

"I don't like to talk about it."

Veronica looked up at him. "It's okay, you can trust me."

"I wrote to Santa every year until I was twelve. He never answered. He never brought me any presents. I stopped believing in him a long time ago."

Veronica laughed. "What? You know he's real. You just spoke to him!"

"Knowing he's real and believing in him are two different things. Every year I asked for the same thing, but every year I got the shaft, while the other kids in the neighborhood got everything they asked for."

"I'm sorry, Noel."

"Ironic, isn't it? I devote my life protecting a man who never came through for me as a child. It doesn't matter. It was a long time ago and my childhood is over."

"You're never too old to be a child," said Veronica.

Green was quiet for a moment. He felt that maybe he'd gone too far, let her see too much of his private side. He didn't like the way it made him feel, but he was just being honest.

"And aren't you the guy who sold *me* on the North Pole?" asked Veronica.

"Yeah, I did a good sales job. The North Pole is a great place. I know that, but the truth is it's the hardworking people behind the scenes that make Christmas something magical. If you ask me, Santa Claus is kind of just a spokesman. With a PR rep and everything."

Veronica pulled back from Green.

"You don't believe that. You sound like Cole. I don't like this side of you."

Green sighed regretfully. "Neither do I."

The sleigh banked north and flew along the shoreline before turning inland toward the dazzling lights, colossal spires, and lofty structures of brick and steel that were New York City.

"Hold on everyone, we're here," said Winters. He guided the sleigh toward the rooftop of an apartment building.

The reindeer, led by Tinsel, glided onto the roof, hovering and pulling the sleigh with practiced, coordinated movements. Landing Santa's sleigh high above New York City, on a small roof, wasn't an easy process, especially for the B-team, but they put the sleigh down gently, almost without sound. All four passengers exited the sleigh, including Avalanche.

Green covered Tinsel's nose before he, Winters, Veronica, and Avalanche exited the roof via the service door.

As soon as they were gone there was a rustling over by the chimney. A hobo, who had been on the roof the whole time lying underneath the stars, was completely stunned by what he had just witnessed.

He held up a bottle and gave it a strange look.

Inside the apartment building, the four haggard travelers walked slowly down the hallway. The elevator doors opened and an elderly man holding a newspaper stepped out. He took one look at Avalanche and froze.

Green and company smiled, trying to act nonchalant, but Avalanche let out an enormous roar. The old man squealed and high-tailed it back into the elevator, dropping his newspaper.

"We've got to get him out of sight," said Green.

They came to the apartment where the Clauses were staying. Green knocked on the door.

"Baruch Hashem!" said Santa as he opened the door. "Come on in!"

Green shook his head at Santa's Yiddish phrasing as he led Veronica, Winters, and Avalanche inside the tiny apartment.

"Oy vey!" said Santa at the sight of Avalanche.

"Don't worry, sir," said Winters, "he's a friend of ours. He won't harm you."

"Well, in that case, shalom, my giant friend. Ho ho ho!" Santa rubbed Avalanche's tummy and the giant beast smiled and giggled.

Mrs. Claus walked over to the old radio and turned it down.

"Well, it looks like you two have really taken to your cover," said Green.

"Such wonderful Menschen, these Jewish people are," said Santa.

"I think he just might convert!" said Mrs. Claus.

Veronica laughed. "That might be a conflict of interest."

Santa chuckled. "You all look exhausted. Better rest up. We have a big day tomorrow."

"Not until I give you a full report, sir," said Green.

The smile left Santa's face. "Of course."

CHAPTER EIGHTEEN

The apartment was dark. Green and Winters slept in sleeping bags on the floor. Veronica was on the sofa under a quilt with images of dreidels and menorahs stitched into it.

Veronica watched Green sleep. She couldn't stop thinking about their conversation. It pained her to think that Green felt the way he did about Santa. She wished there was something she could do to heal Green, help him believe in Santa as she did.

Avalanche lay on the floor close to Veronica, his monstrous snoring rumbling the couch.

Veronica heard a noise from the kitchen. Curiosity and the need to investigate overtook her. She climbed off the sofa and tiptoed across the living room. Peering around the corner, she found Santa sitting at the table with milk and cookies. The fridge door was wide open.

"Santa?"

Santa jumped and spilled milk onto his lap. "Whoa, ho, ho." Santa looked down at his midnight snack. "She wouldn't make them if she didn't want me to eat them."

Veronica smiled.

"Can't sleep?" asked Santa.

She shook her head.

Santa could tell something was bothering her. He moved to invite her over, and she joined him at the table. "What is it, dear?"

"Something I heard today has been on my mind," said Veronica.

"Anything I can help you with?"

"Actually, yes. Santa . . . why do you have a naughty list?"

Santa nodded. This was a question he had heard many times

before. He patted her hand. "The naughty list is not quite what people think it is. It's actually the kids on the naughty list I pay the most attention to."

"But you don't give them presents."

Santa turned to Veronica. His eyes were warm and filled with compassion. "Oh no, my dear. Ho, ho. I give presents to all of them, everyone who asks me. Though it may not always be exactly what they ask me for."

"But there are kids you don't bring gifts to, aren't there? Even kids who write to you?" asked Veronica.

Sadness filled Santa's eyes. "Yes, that is true. I bring gifts into every home where I am invited. But I can't force gifts on anyone; that would violate the spirit of Christmas. There are some kids who miss out, even ones who write to me. That's why I do appearances like the Macy's Parade. It's to give those kids a chance to see me, even for just a few minutes."

"We could let people know that," said Veronica.

"Yes, and we could let them know that when I used to deliver coal to families in the winter it was a blessing, not a punishment! Coal was a valued commodity; it helped people heat their homes. I was helping those families stay warm during long, cold winters. But I can't explain away all of the preconceptions people have about me. In some ways, it's not my place to try to explain to the world what I'm doing. People have their own traditions that are very meaning-ful. I have my role, *my* traditions, but I am not the be-all and end-all of Christmas."

"You're not?"

Santa smiled. "Ho, ho, Christmas is about so much more than an old man in a red suit."

Veronica thought about that. "You tried telling me this before. You said it's about gifts and the hope they can bring."

"There is nothing better than a gift well given."

"It's all about *giving*."

"Yes, and it's symbolic of something bigger than ourselves," said Santa. "The greatest gift."

Veronica nodded. Finally she understood. Christmas was the holiday and it existed independent of Santa Claus. It was celebrated for different reasons by different people. Santa was simply someone who did something selfless on that day, albeit on a massive and mind-boggling scale. He celebrated the Christmas holiday by giving to everyone he could.

She'd never thought of Christmas or Santa Claus in quite those terms before. She no longer felt like a woman in her thirties. She felt like a kid again. She was sitting in a kitchen with Santa—*the* Santa Claus!

"Santa?"

"Yes, Veronica?"

"Where do you come from? I mean, I know some of the stories, Saint Nicholas, Father Christmas, but who are you?"

Santa put down his milk. "No one knows my story. Not my full story. And it's not really important who I am. It's what I do that's important. One day I will tell you and Noel about all of it. In fact, I'll *show* you. But it's not something that's appropriate to speak of at this moment."

"I don't understand," said Veronica.

"I know that. But you have to trust me. You have to believe that everything I do is for the best.

"Right now, it's best that I simply tell you that once I was lost; once I knew not the path I should travel. Once I was simply a man looking for a meaningful purpose. And, Veronica, I found it. I have one purpose."

Santa's eyes twinkled with joy. "Everything I do, all of it, the North Pole, the sleigh, the reindeer, the gifts, everything is to bring hope and joy into the hearts of the children of the world who I love so very much."

Tears filled Veronica's eyes. She reached up and hugged Santa, hugged him as tight as a toddler would cling to her father. "I love you, Santa."

"Thank you, Veronica. I've always known."

Santa wiped Veronica's tears away.

PART THREE

CHAPTER NINETEEN

Rowland Hussey Macy started many retail stores, including the very first Macy's in Haverhill, Massachusetts. He didn't have much success until 1858 when he opened a store called R.H. Macy's & Co. in New York City. The store was an immediate success and grew into a chain of stores throughout the city. In 1902, the store's flagship location moved to Herald Square, on 34th Street.

By the 1920s Macy's department stores were a well-known and respected brand. Many of their employees were first generation immigrants from Europe. These workers loved their new country and wanted to put together a celebration much like the festivals that were familiar in cities throughout Europe. They got together and convinced the store's management to stage a parade that would end at the store's 34th Street location.

The first parade was in 1924 and was called the Macy's Christmas Parade. The parade was a spectacle with floats, live acts, and animals from the Central Park Zoo. Over a quarter of a million people watched the parade, which ended with a special guest being introduced at Herald Square. At that first parade, and every Macy's parade after that, Santa Claus closed the show, symbolizing the start of the Christmas season. The parade was a success and quickly became an American tradition, viewed by millions of people every Thanksgiving. It was not an event that Santa Claus would miss.

Excited crowds were gathered up and down 77th Street and Central Park West, alive with anticipation and wonder, waiting for the Macy's Thanksgiving Day Parade to begin.

There was a mass of elaborate floats featuring characters from

Frozen, Tangled, and Iron Man. Tethered to the floats were larger-than-life balloons of Snoopy, Garfield, SpongeBob, and comic book heroes like Batman and Superman. Marching bands, dancers, and furry mascots from movies and TV took their places as the show was about to begin.

Green, wearing a black suit, sunglasses, and his candy cane pin, watched over the area as they prepared to bring Santa to his float, which was a replica of his sleigh.

Green spoke to a policeman, Officer Lyon. "I assume that your captain has briefed you and your men about the recent threats on Mr. Claus. Is that right?"

"Must have told us, oh I don't know, a billion times. I don't know who we're supposed to pay more attention to, Santa or Justin Timberlake."

"Timberlake, eh? Never head of him," said Green.

"Where have you been?"

"Up north, Officer Lyon, up north."

Lyon laughed; many officers in the NYPD had long known that Santa Claus, at least the one who rode in the Macy's parade, was real. It was a badge of honor to be one of the officers on security detail during the parade.

Over by the prep area for the floats, Winters strutted through rows of the giant traveling stages. Thousands of performers were making final preparations. Winters waved at an all-girls drill team, and some of the girls giggled and waved back.

Green called in over the radio. "Winters, are all assigned SSS personnel present and accounted for?"

"Yes, sir! Everyone is positioned at their assigned posts."

"Copy that. Keep a sharp eye out," said Green over the radio.

"You and Miss Snow got pretty comfortable in the back of the sleigh last night. Are you two an item yet?"

"Stay focused, Winters! We need to keep a lookout out for Cole and Frostbite."

"Yes, sir. Where is the big guy now?"

"Getting touch ups in the make-up trailer; those cheeks don't stay *that* rosy all by themselves."

Winters stood in line at a Starbucks coffee cart. He noticed a beautiful TV news reporter throwing her hands up in frustration at the press table nearby.

"Stop the presses," said Winters, under his breath.

Winters made his way over to the table, flashing his badge. "What seems to be the problem?"

The reporter turned to Winters. It was Ivy holding a microphone. He saw her and she saw him and neither one of them was embarrassed by how long they stared into each other's eyes.

A parade attendant shook his head. "This woman claims to be press, but says she forgot her credentials."

Ivy and Winters continued starring at each other. "I can vouch for her. She's with me," he said without looking away from Ivy.

"Fine," said the attendant. "I haven't got all day. Name?"

Ivy finally turned. "What? Oh, it's Heather! Heather Smith, and my cameraman Leroy . . . Frost."

Winters smiled. "Well, Miss Smith. Let's remember your credentials next time."

"Yes, of course, sir."

The attendant handed Ivy two badges. Ivy and Winters left the press table together.

"I must have left my press pass on the train or something. I feel like such a space cadet. Thank you!" said Ivy, giving Winters a small, friendly hug of appreciation.

"My pleasure. The only thing I'd ask from you in return is that you tell me what channel you're on. If I'd known you were doing the news, I'd be a frequent viewer. I only watch *Top Gear*."

"Action 6 News at . . . six, yeah, on channel, uh, six. I'm Heather Smith."

"Isaac Winters. Can I buy you a cup of coffee, Miss Smith? I mean Heather."

They walked toward the coffee cart and a barista asked, "What can I get you?"

"We'll take two peppermint lattes," said Winters.

"Two peppermint lattes, coming up."

Ivy gasped; it had been a long time since she'd had something sweet. "Peppermint latte? Sounds scrumptious."

"You've never had one? They're like liquid candy."

"Confession, I don't usually do the whole holiday thing. This is new territory for me," said Ivy.

The barista handed Winters and Ivy their lattes and they took a sip.

"Mmmm! Oh my goodness, that is good!" said Ivy, smiling up at Winters.

"That oughta keep you warm, Miss Smith. Well, I'd better get back. The parade is about to begin."

"I saw you flash a badge back there. Just whom do you work for?" asked Ivy.

"Let's just say I'm part of a team here to make sure one of the world's most beloved figures isn't harmed," said Winters.

"Justin Timberlake?"

"Close."

Winters pulled out a business card and handed it to Ivy. "You call me if these guys give you any more trouble, or if there's anything else I can do with you . . . for you."

Ivy blushed. "I'll be sure to let you know if I think of something."

"I'm glad we met," said Winters.

"Oh, yes," said Ivy. "Happy to have met you too."

Winters took her hand and gave it a small kiss before walking away.

Ivy smiled wide for the first time in years. She looked down at the business card and quickly realized whom Winters worked for.

She looked up in time to see him disappear into the crowd as she tapped his card against her palm.

Cole's sleigh sat atop an old skyscraper. The wolves gnawed on raw meat during their downtime.

The service door opened, and Ivy joined Cole and Frostbite on the roof. She carried her microphone and a cup of coffee. Frostbite was dressed as a cameraman and he held an enormous, old school film camera.

"What took you so long?" asked Cole.

"Starbucks always has a huge line," said Ivy.

"Did you get me a rotten milk latte?"

"They refused to make it."

"Fine. Give me whatever that is then." Cole snatched the coffee right out of Ivy's hands and took a small sip. He immediately recoiled, spewing the beverage all over Frostbite.

"Yuck! Is that peppermint?"

"Yeah, I guess so. Thought you might want to try something new."

Cole whipped the hot drink over his shoulder, and it crashed into Frostbite, splattering all over his jacket.

"It reeks of holiday cheer. Disgusting!" Cole licked his sleeve, trying to get the taste out. "Is everything set?" he asked, gathering himself.

"Of course. I got us a great spot close to the anchor desk." Ivy handed Frostbite his press badge and pinned her own badge to her lapel.

"Well done, Ivy. Millions will witness the end of Claus's reign on live television," cackled Cole. He turned to Frostbite, who was wiping the coffee off. "And what about you, coffee stains? Is that thing armed?"

"Not yet, sir," said Frostbite. He opened the side of the camera, revealing a compartment filled with water and a canister of gas.

Frostbite pressed a few buttons, then slipped the cover back on.

"Are you sure you want to do this?" asked Ivy.

"Are you nuts? Of course I do!" said Cole. "You just have a case of the pre-assassination jitters. But don't worry, my pet, everything is going to be fine."

He reached out his hand, "Bring your hands in."

Ivy and Frostbite reluctantly placed their hands over Cole's as he let out a cheer, "Go evil!" They threw their hands in the air, Ivy visibly conflicted.

SSS personnel worked over last minute inspections to Santa's float, thoroughly checking the sleigh for any contraband or explosives. Rudolph and the A-team were attached to the re-creation of Santa's sleigh in the center of the float.

Cody tended to the reindeer in a makeshift stable area for Tinsel and the B-team. Santa's real sleigh was parked close by, watched over by Cliff and Biff.

Green led Mr. and Mrs. Claus and Veronica to the float.

"Okay, sir, I'm giving you an all clear to board the float as soon as you're ready," said Green

"Ho, ho, ho, thank you, Agent Green!"

"Enjoy your parade, sir."

"This is one of my favorite days!" said Santa.

"Okay, you two. Let's get you boarded," said Green

Green saw Santa and Mrs. Claus up onto the float as he and Veronica stood back.

"Noel, I'm sorry about last night," said Veronica.

"For what?"

"I was a little insensitive. I always had wonderful Christmases, so it's hard for me to imagine someone not liking Christmas."

"I've been thinking about what I said last night as well. And you know something? Having you be a part of this, getting to see all of it through your eyes helps me appreciate it."

Veronica gave him a peck on the cheek.

Green looked over at her, his eyes filled with something more than friendship. He gathered himself, maintaining his composure. "So, where's Avalanche?"

"He's safe in one of our unmarked vehicles. I just bought him some cotton candy, so he's very happy."

Avalanche sat in the back seat of a Chevy Suburban. He enjoyed a giant spool of pink cotton candy. "Yuh - mee - yum - yum! Can - dee - caught - in!"

He licked his fingers, gleeful in sugary bliss.

Outside, on the street, Frostbite and Ivy hustled to their positions. Frostbite was a few yards ahead of Ivy.

"Frostbite, wait up. I can't walk that fast," said Ivy. "These heels were not designed for speed, buster."

Frostbite stopped next to the black Chevy Suburban parked along the sidewalk. He saw in the reflection of one of the tinted rear windows that he was still covered in coffee. He tried to wipe it off, but it was a wasted effort. He sighed as Ivy caught up.

Inside the Suburban, Avalanche saw Frostbite and cowered, not realizing that Frostbite couldn't see anything through the tinted windows.

Ivy stood next to Frostbite and also checked her reflection in the tinted window. "How do I look?"

"Like a reporter, ma'am," said Frostbite.

Cole called in over the radio to earpieces that Ivy and Frostbite both wore. "Are you two in position yet?"

"No, sir," said Frostbite, speaking into a pin in the shape of an S with an arrow pointing down. "Miss Ivy's shoes are slowing her down."

Ivy smacked Frostbite's arm for throwing her under the bus.

* * *

Up above, Cole peered over the edge of the building to the parade route below. He looked into a small handheld monitor that fed him an image from Frostbite's camera.

"Hey, pasty face, let's see some picture. I don't want to miss a thing!" Cole said over the radio.

Frostbite's voice came back, "One moment, sir."

After a few moments, Cole's monitor came alive. "Have you tried that thing out yet?" asked Cole.

"No, sir," said Frostbite.

"Don't you think that might be a good idea?"

Frostbite moved into an alley, Ivy right behind him. He pressed a button and the camera lens slid back, revealing a gun barrel. He turned around and fired a practice round into a graffiti-covered wall. An ice bullet vaporized against the concrete.

Frostbite spoke into his pin. "It works! Ice bullets were a brilliant idea, sir."

"Of course they were; I'm a genius! Now get moving!"

Frostbite clutched his camera and moved back out of the alley with Ivy struggling to keep up.

Inside the Suburban, Avalanche had seen everything and tried to duck down below the window out of view, which was essentially impossible given his large frame. "Uh oh! Baaaaaahd!"

Ahead, on a cross street, the Macy's Thanksgiving Day Parade marshal waved a baton in the air and blew a whistle, signaling the start of the festivities.

CHAPTER TWENTY

Roger Carlisle, early sixties, and Olivia Brian, late thirties, were national cable television personalities. They sat behind an anchor desk staged above the parade route, wired for sound and happily broadcasting live coverage of the parade.

"Happy Thanksgiving and welcome to the Macy's Thanksgiving Day Parade! I'm Roger Carlisle, and with me as always is my lovely cohost, Olivia Brian."

"Happy Thanksgiving!" said Olivia. "Thanks for tuning in. It's a cold morning here in Manhattan. They're saying we could see some snow today."

"Boy, wouldn't that add to the holiday spirit?" asked Roger. "Be sure to stay with us throughout our coverage; there's bound to be a few surprises. We'll be right back after this."

Their station broke away from live coverage for commercials. The two anchors lost their happy, cheesy demeanors. Olivia pulled out a giant cup of coffee and took a huge gulp.

"Oh boy, I needed that," said Olivia.

Roger looked Olivia up and down. "Late night? You're a mess, Olivia."

"Stuff it, Roger!" said Olivia, taking another gulp of her coffee.

Parade floats got their name from early European parades where the main events were large displays built on barges, which were pulled along canals or rivers. The Macy's parade was world famous for the floats and spectacular balloons that would wind their way down the historic parade route. And as tradition held, the final float in the parade featured Santa Claus.

Santa and Mrs. Claus sat in the replica sleigh featured on that year's float. The entire reindeer A-team was positioned in front. Rudolph's nose was covered to protect the audience's vision.

Green walked along one side of the float and Winters was on the other. They carefully assessed the crowd, looking for any danger.

"I'm telling you, Green, this chick I just met is smokin'!" said Winters over his SSS communications pin. Green and Winters spoke through a private channel.

Green put his hand to his ear and spoke through his candy cane pin. "Who?"

"I ran into this tasty television reporter. I think I'm in love."

"With a girl you *just* met?"

"Well, excuse me if I don't need to wait an entire year before I ask a girl out. Haven't you ever heard of love at first sight?"

"Yeah. I've also heard of the Loch Ness Monster. Doesn't mean it exists."

"Those are strong words coming from a man who works for Santa Claus," said Winters. "Open your mind, man. Nothing amazing in life happens without believing first."

"Thanks, Mr. Rogers. Now, let's cut the radio chatter," said Green out loud. In his head, though, he knew there was some truth in Winters's words.

"I'm just saying, take a leap, buddy, and tell her you love her already."

Green was silent.

"Life doesn't bring you a girl like Miss Snow every day."

As Green cased the crowd he spotted Veronica standing in the VIP booth. She saw him and smiled, giving a small wave. Green smiled back and nodded.

Frostbite and Ivy were set up like a typical cameraman and news anchor with a clear, unobstructed view of the parade.

Frostbite filmed Ivy as she pretended to do a "stand-up" facing the camera, holding her microphone. Over her shoulder, Santa's float slowly approached, still several hundred yards away.

On the rooftop, Cole watched his handheld monitor, barely able to contain his excitement. Although there had been setbacks, his plans were finally going to come to fruition, and Santa was finally going to be out of the picture.

"Here they come. Get ready," he said to Ivy and Frostbite over their radios. Cole closed his eyes and imagined a day when his float would end the parade, when kids would yell his name and beg him for presents.

Down on the street, Ivy was growing worried. "What about those SSS guys? We're not going to hurt them, are we?"

"If they get in our way, I'll take out those sugarplummin' Northies too," said Frostbite.

Ivy looked down the street and saw Santa's float, with Winters alongside it, coming their way.

Frostbite turned to look at the float with his camera, and when he turned back, Ivy was gone. Her microphone sat on the ground. Frostbite frantically scanned the crowd, but he lost her in the sea of people.

Cole screamed as his view on the monitor pointed to the ground. "What are you doing?"

Frostbite came back over the radio. "Boss, I think we have a problem! Ivy's gone!"

Winters looked over the crowd for possible threats when Ivy appeared, heading in his direction and waving her arms at him. "Heather?"

Ivy yelled over the noise of the crowd. "Agent Winters!"

Winters smiled and waved.

Ivy neared the float.

"Green?" Winters said via his candy cane pin.

Green looked over at Winters. "What is it?"

"The girl I was telling you about."

"Come on, man, I get that you're in love, but we need to focus here," said Green.

Winters turned and saw Ivy's panicked expression and sensed trouble. "No, listen, Noel. She's at two o'clock, signaling me. Something's wrong here. I'm going to check it out."

"Roger that," said Green.

Winters broke his stride and pushed into the crowd toward Ivy. He held his badge up and instructed people to let him through.

Ivy saw him coming and turned to find Santa's float getting closer to Frostbite's position. She was frozen with worry.

Winters made it to Ivy through the thick crowd. "Heather, what's wrong?" he shouted, trying to be heard above the din of the crowd.

"My name isn't Heather; it's Ivy. You have to stop this parade!"

"What? Why?"

"They're going to hurt Santa Claus."

"Who?" Winters grabbed Ivy.

Ivy pointed toward a crowd of Network cameramen. "One of those cameramen is going to take a shot at Santa with an ice bullet! You can't let that happen!"

Winters looked ahead and quickly sized up the situation.

"I'm sorry, Agent Winters," said Ivy. "I work for Cole."

Out of nowhere, Cole appeared behind Winters. He had on a black cloak with a hood to hide his face, and he held a Taser in his right hand.

"Not any more, you don't," shrieked Cole.

Before Winters could turn, Cole zapped him. Winters went limp and fell to the ground. Cole stuck the weapon into Ivy's side and pushed himself up next to her.

"I would have never taken you for a Northie sympathizer," he whispered sharply into her ear. "What a waste. Now get moving, my dear."

Cole shoved Ivy through the crowd and into an alley.

Beside the float, Green searched the crowd for Winters. "Winters! Where are you?" he spoke via his candy cane pin. "Come in, Agent Winters! Do you copy?"

Santa's float neared the press area. Frostbite stood at the center of the line of cameramen, the camera mounted on his shoulder. His eye was on the viewfinder, and he moved the camera to face directly at the approaching float. He could see Santa smiling and waving to the crowd. He flicked a switch and crosshairs locked on Santa Claus.

In the alley close by, Cole watched the monitor. His eyes widened. "Yes, that's it!"

The float was almost directly in front of Frostbite's location, which was just below the anchor desk where Roger and Olivia sat up in their chairs, watching and providing a play-by-play for the audience at home.

"Now wait a moment, what's this we're getting from camera 3?" asked Roger.

On the monitor for camera 3, Roger and Olivia watched as a massive white beast raced through the crowd, shoving on-lookers out of the way as he made a beeline toward Santa's float.

Olivia shook her head in bewilderment. "It looks like the Abominable Snowman!"

"Well, what do the folks from the North Pole have in store for us this year?" asked Roger, thinking Avalanche was a part of the show.

Down on the street, the crowd was starting to get the sense that Avalanche was not a part of the show. Avalanche barreled for Santa's float. Frightened patrons screamed as they darted out of his way. Two NYPD officers tried seizing him. "Freeze! Stay where you are!"

Avalanche sent them flying through the air with a simple swipe of his arm.

Next to the float, Green saw Avalanche running straight for them. Green scanned the crowd for the danger that must have provoked the white beast. His eyes traveled over the area where all of the cameramen stood. One of the cameras was larger and much older than the others. Everything seemed to slow down as Green zeroed in on Frostbite.

"Code red! Code red!" Green shouted into his pin. "Protect the Beard!" Green ran toward Frostbite, and then realized he was the only agent close enough to Santa to protect him. He drew his Freeze Ray, turning back toward the float.

Frostbite had Santa perfectly aligned in the crosshairs. He had a clear shot.

Green knew he wasn't going to make it up on to the float in time. He swiveled and took aim at Frostbite and fired. Frostbite dropped to the ground and green lightning hit a crosswalk light just behind him, showering sparks into the crowd.

Avalanche tumbled through a marching band, sending band members and instruments flying.

Frostbite barely flinched as sparks rained down behind him. He repositioned and took aim.

On the float, Santa stopped waving and turned to the commotion.

In the alley, Cole's eyes widened as he watched via his monitor. "Do it! Now!"

Frostbite's finger slowly pressed the trigger. The weapon fired, and the ice bullet was forced out of the barrel of the camera gun by a powerful burst of gas. It flew toward Santa's float.

"No!" shouted Green.

As he reached the float, Avalanche hurled himself through the air. He landed directly in front of Santa Claus as the bullet slammed directly into the beast's chest. Avalanche fell onto the edge of the float and rolled directly in front of Santa and Mrs. Claus.

In the alley, Cole jumped up and down in anger and frustration. "No, no, no!"

Green jumped on the float, yelling into his pin, "Shots fired, shots fired!" He took a protective position in front of the Clauses. "Sir, ma'am, are you all right?"

"We're fine," said Santa. "But I don't know about our big friend here. He took the hit for us, Green."

Green turned and spoke into his pin, "This is a level one emergency! Escort the Clauses to safety. I'm pursuing the shooter. Get a medic to the scene immediately. We have an injured party. I want him treated right away! Over."

Veronica ran toward the float from the VIP booth. She leapt on to the float and dropped next to Avalanche. She threw her arms around him. "Somebody help him!"

Green saw Frostbite with his camera slacked to his side, several yards ahead of the float. Frostbite locked eyes with Green for a brief moment. Then he dropped the camera and took off running. Green sprinted after him.

At the anchor desk, Roger and Olivia were up on their feet looking over the scene below.

"Wow!" said Olivia. "What an interesting bit of theatrics coming from the North Pole this year."

"You can say that again, Olivia," said Roger. "Stay tuned. When we return, there's bound to be plenty more surprises."

They went to commercial and the anchors relaxed.

"This is all staged, right?" asked Olivia.

"It wasn't on the program, but it's got to be," said Roger.

"Weird direction they're going in this year! Interesting, but weird."

CHAPTER TWENTY-ONE

Winters lay on the ground, unconscious. He opened his eyes and put a hand to the bump on his head as he came to slowly, unsure of where he was or what had happened. He pushed himself to his feet, trying to gain his bearings. "Heather? Ivy!"

Winters quickly realized that a sea of chaos and panic surrounded him. SSS agents and NYPD officers were working frantically to secure a perimeter around Santa's float. The crowd was scattering, hurriedly fleeing the area.

Winters checked that his SSS pin was intact. "Green, this is Winters, do you copy?"

Green came back over the radio, "Where have you been?"

"Cole's here! He zapped me. I've been out cold. What happened? Has Mr. Claus been injured?"

"Negative! Avalanche took the hit and saved Mr. Claus's life," said Green.

"What's your twenty, sir?"

"I'm on foot in pursuit of Frostbite, north up the parade route. I'm almost back to base camp."

"Copy that, Green! I'm on my way." Winters flagged down an NYPD officer on horseback. He extended his badge in the air. "Agent Winters of the SSS, I'm going to need to commandeer your horse!"

"Yes, sir," said the officer as he dismounted.

Winters hopped up on the horse. "Yaw!" He spurred the horse on with a quick squeeze of his calves and they took off.

Further back up the parade route, the rest of the crowd was slower to react. Some of them moved out of the way as Green chased Frostbite. Frostbite knocked others over as he raced for Central Park.

Snow began to fall as Green trailed Frostbite into the park. He lost him in the vast expanse of trees and bushes. Green stood still, trying to discern where Frostbite could have gone. A few moments passed and Green didn't see any signs of him.

Green jumped back as Cole's sleigh and wolf team burst from behind a cluster of trees. Frostbite was in the sleigh along with Ivy and Cole. He smiled and waved at Green as they took off into the sky.

Green swiveled around and raced for base camp.

Winters rode up on horseback as Green reached the starting point of the parade where Santa's sleigh was being watched over by other agents.

"I just saw them; they flew right over me!" exclaimed Winters.

"I know, I know!"

Green sprinted toward Santa's sleigh. Winters jumped off the horse and followed him.

Cody was working to secure the B-team to the sleigh. "I just heard the news, thought I'd get them ready."

Green kissed Cody on the head. "Cody, you are a blessing straight from heaven. Are they ready to go?"

"Heck yeah they are!"

Green and Winters jumped in the sleigh, and Cody removed the cover from Tinsel's nose.

"Yeeaw!" Green commanded the reindeer and pulled on the reins. Hovering slowly into the air, they were soon clear of the trees and buildings. Green cracked the reins and the reindeer lowered their heads and launched into the sky in pursuit of Cole.

Up in the air, the snow came down harder and the speed of the reindeer made visibility less than perfect. Green maneuvered Santa's sleigh high above the streets of Manhattan with the green glow from Tinsel illuminating the way.

Cole's sleigh was ahead in the distance, in a canyon made of skyscrapers. Green pushed the reindeer, knowing that it was risky, but fully intent on closing the gap.

Ahead, Cole turned back and saw Green and Winters approaching. He made a sharp turn, flying over a street that was full of parade floats and giant balloons. Cole pulled tight on the reins, urging his wolves on. They weaved through the tops of the large balloons.

Green made the same sharp turns, the sleigh inches from ramming into an enormous balloon in the shape of Charlie Brown's head.

"Balloons! Watch out for the balloons!" shouted Winters.

Green whipped the reins as they rounded a building, nearly flipping onto their side. They flew out from behind the building and barely avoided a collision with a massive Yo Gabba Gabba! balloon.

"That was close!" yelled Green.

"Yeah! Be careful!" said Winters. "I don't want to be taken out by a giant one-eyed monster."

The two sleighs roared toward the Empire State Building. The building's tenants rushed to their windows to view the amazing spectacle.

Cole's sleigh made a sudden dip, racing almost straight down toward the street below, the wolves pulling them into a tight dive. Ivy clutched the seat back and held on for dear life.

Santa's sleigh steered down in the same dive. Tinsel's nose shone brightly as the reindeers inched closer to Cole.

Just before it crashed into the street, Cole's sleigh whipped to the left, disappearing around the base of the Empire State Building.

Green pulled Santa's sleigh out of the dive, but missed the turn that Cole had made. Green and Winters turned and watched Cole speeding back up into the sky.

"They're getting away!" yelled Winters.

"Hang on to something!" Green shouted.

Green pulled hard on the reins. The reindeer turned sharply and flew just above the tops of cars. Green and Winters couldn't see any trace of Cole's sleigh.

"Where did they go? Did we lose them?" wondered Winters.

Green called up a three-dimensional map of New York City on the display on the sleigh's dash. He could see a blinking image representing Cole's sleigh pulling far away from the city.

"We're never going to catch up. He's got too much of a head start and those dogs are too fast." Green thought for a moment, and then pushed a button that opened the Time Expander controls.

"Hold on," said Winters. "You're not thinking about cranking that up, are you?"

"It's the only way! He's as good as gone unless we use it!"

"Yeah but the technology is, you know, dangerous, right? Do you even know how it works?"

"Not really. But Santa's given me a brief overview. I think I remember how it goes."

"Yeah, punching a hole in the universe to slow time to a dead crawl? Piece of cake."

"We have to try it. Cole used lethal force! He crossed a line, Isaac. He crossed a line, and he's not getting away! This ends now!" Green narrowed his eyes as he pressed a sequence of buttons to initiate the Time Expander.

CHAPTER TWENTY-TWO

There are many stories that explain the origins of Santa Claus, though his real story has not been told. Many of the stories about Saint Nicholas or Sinterklaas, Tomte from Nordic folklore, Odin from German folklore, and Father Christmas, influenced Santa and inspired him to become what the world now knew him as.

Santa was a real person. His given name was Kristopher Kringle. He was born in 1733 in a Scandinavian colony in Greenland.

Kris's parents were Christian missionaries sent there from Denmark to help convert the native population. When he was a small boy his parents died from smallpox, which also claimed the rest of the colony. Kris wasn't infected, and it was thought that there was something special about him, that there must have been a reason he was spared from the disease. This led a group of Viking explorers to believe that he was blessed, and they claimed him as a kind of good luck charm.

Kris began exploring when he was only nine years old. He became an expert in topography and navigation, and by the time he was in his twenties, he was one of the leaders in a fleet of Viking exploratory ships.

But Kris longed for something more. He had always thought that he had a purpose, some reason for being that went beyond reading maps and searching for habitable land. Something always pulled him north. Maybe it was the memory of his parents and their time together in Greenland, he wasn't sure, but he knew that he needed to go as far north as he could.

This eventually led to his personal exploration of the North Pole, his encounters with the First Knights of the Pole, the Blue Witch, and the events that led to him becoming Santa Claus and living beyond the grasp of illness or aging with Mrs. Claus.

For there was real magic behind all of the mysteries of the North Pole that Santa had access to. But it took him many years to learn how to blend the magic of the Pole with science. The magic of the Pole wasn't the kind where you could snap your fingers and stop time. It had to work within the laws and boundaries of nature and science. As Santa began bringing gifts to the children of the world, the flying reindeer were his first magical advantage and this was done mostly in Scandinavia.

As time went on and the idea of Santa Claus and his role in Christmas spread to other areas of the world, Kris wanted to be able to expand his capacity. He worked with some of the most brilliant minds of their eras. But it wasn't until he met Nikola Tesla that he was able to fully harness the magic of the Pole and meld it with the technological advances Tesla had invented.

Nikola Tesla was born in 1856 in the Austrian Empire. He crossed paths with Kris in Prague in 1880 when Tesla was attending classes at a university there. Kris recognized the brilliance of Tesla and shared with him the developmental stages of the Time Expander. Tesla wrestled with the problem of how to perfect the mechanisms of the Time Expander so that it could allow Santa to travel at incredible speeds without hurting him.

This was something Tesla worked on in secret as his career took off. He worked on other projects with Thomas Edison and then on his own, inventing items others got credit for including the radio, radar, and x-rays, but because of his fascination with the Time Expander, Tesla never cared or fought for acclaim and adulation. Tesla was selfless, and his true joy came from solving problems and improving the lives of others.

Tesla finally solved the issues with the Time Expander in 1899 in Colorado Springs where he was perfecting his work on alternating currents (even producing artificial lightning). There were many rumors in Colorado Springs about strange things happening at Tesla's lab there, including incredible lights, flying deer, and a magic sleigh.

Tesla had created a functional Time Expander. At the turn of the century, Santa began to take advantage of it, always remembering to follow Tesla's specific instructions because, as Tesla had warned him, the Time Expander could be altered to use the force of its power as a weapon on an atomic level.

Green knew almost nothing of this history as he pressed the sequence of buttons on the Time Expander control panel. All he was thinking about was catching Cole.

"Strap in and man up," said Green to Winters.

The Time Expander screen displayed an array of complex equations, numbers, and symbols flashing by rapidly. Winters shot Green a worried look. "You have any idea what that stuff means?"

"None!" yelled Green.

The Time Expander screen flashed red, reading *Initiating Continuum Breach.* Everything around the sleigh and reindeer, including the air, seemed to bend and there was a loud humming noise. The sleigh was sucked violently into a vortex created directly in front of Tinsel.

As the sleigh pierced the vortex there was an intense flash of bright white light and the sleigh vanished, leaving waves of distortion in its wake.

In Cole's sleigh, he, Frostbite, and Ivy were all sitting quietly, the sleigh sailing through the sky at a quick but even pace. Cole laughed.

"Lost 'em! Those gift-wrapped wieners!" Cole clapped his hands.

"I don't know what you're so happy about," said Ivy. "They stopped you. You failed." She was worried about Winters and felt horrible about being associated with the attempt on Santa.

Cole's enthusiasm was replaced with a look of disgust. "Thanks for reminding me of that, my dear. It wasn't just Green and his team of cocoa-drinking clowns that managed to screw up my brilliant plan. They had some help, didn't they?"

Ivy moved away from Cole, trying to disappear in a corner of the sleigh. "What are you going to do to me, Cole?"

Cole looked over at Frostbite. "I don't know. Frostbite, what do you think we should do with her?"

Frostbite grinned; his teeth were all sharp—like a shark's. "I think we should take her and—"

"Shut up, you overgrown snow blower," said Cole. "I was being rhetorical. I don't care what you think."

Frostbite stopped grinning.

"You know, in old nautical times, if a member of the crew was deemed treasonous, they would walk the plank. Or, if they didn't have a plank, they would toss them overboard," said Cole as he looked around for something. "Hmmm . . . doesn't look like we brought our plank. Oh well, we'll just have to toss you overboard. So sorry, my dear."

Ivy panicked, clutching onto her seat.

"Frostbite, will you do the honors?"

Frostbite grinned and moved toward Ivy.

Inside Santa's sleigh, Winters and Green stared out in wonder as the world outside stood at a standstill. Every flake of falling snow was suspended in mid-air.

Santa's sleigh flew right past a Boeing 747 as if it were frozen in place. Winters peered into the airplane windows. He could see the people inside appeared to be frozen in time. A flight attendant poured a can of Coke over ice, the liquid suspended mid-air as a baby cried, its face scrunched in seemingly eternal agony.

"This is creepy, man. Everything and everyone seems frozen in time, but to them—"

"We are invisible to everybody else," said Green. "We're traveling faster than light. To them everything is completely normal; if their eyes were quickened and they could see us it would blow their minds. But they aren't actually frozen."

Winters extended his arm, almost outside of the sleigh, trying to touch the waves of distortion.

"Stop!" said Green. "If anything within this field were to breach the effects of the Time Expander, it would be pulled back into real time at a dangerous speed."

Winters yanked his arm back into the sleigh. Up ahead, Green spotted Cole's sleigh suspended in the air.

"I've got you now, you rotten milk–drinking assassin," said Green.

"So, what are we going to do?" asked Winters.

"I'm gonna breach and clip their sleigh! At the speed we're going, they won't know what hit 'em."

"Is that safe? Didn't you just tell me not to do that?" asked Winters, his thoughts traveling to the black-haired beauty.

"If we breach inside the sleigh, we'll be fine. This is going to work! Hold on!"

Winters held on and hoped Ivy would be OK.

In Cole's sleigh, Frostbite picked up Ivy. She screamed for her life and kicked and squirmed, trying to break free.

"Please, Cole, don't do this! Please!"

Frostbite hefted Ivy up over the side, setting his feet to throw her out of the sleigh. His grip loosened.

"Wait!" shouted Ivy.

Frostbite paused; it was just enough to save Ivy's life, as there was a loud whoosh and a sudden, powerful jolt against Cole's sleigh. All three passengers were knocked down. The sleigh jerked off course, pulling the team of wolves to and fro, like a string fluttering in the wind.

Inside Santa's sleigh, the impact slammed Green and Winters against the dashboard. The controls lit up red and a repeating buzzer sounded.

* * *

In his sleigh, Cole quickly stood and looked around. Frostbite staggered to his feet. Ivy lay on one of the seats, rubbing her head.

"What was that?" asked Frostbite.

"It's Green!" Cole laughed. "Brilliant! Green is using the backup Time Expander built into Fatty's sleigh. He brought it right to me!"

"What are we going to do, boss?"

In Santa's sleigh, Green tried to regain control. Winters looked back over his shoulder, trying to spot Cole.

"That wasn't good, Green, we shot right past them!"

Green hit a button on the dash, turning off the alarm.

"I know! I've got to slow us down. Another blast like that could rip us apart."

Green made adjustments to the controls, slowing the effects of the Time Expander, and then flipped the reins hard. Tinsel quickly held up, slowing, as the distortion outside the vortex began to clear somewhat. The reindeer bit hard against the forces propelling them forward, turning and forcing the sleigh to spin 180 degrees to face Cole's oncoming sleigh.

The movement around them increased as Green cracked the reins, the effects of the Time Expander slowed slightly, but still in effect. "Forward, Tinsel, haw!" They took aim at Cole's sleigh.

Back in his sleigh, Cole sat with the reins in hand, watching the sky carefully like a cat ready to pounce. He spotted a warped blur in the sky approaching. "I see you," he said to himself.

At the last second, Cole whipped his wolves into action putting his sleigh directly in the path of Santa's.

The two sleighs collided, locking runners. Cole's sleigh was pulled into the Time Expander's vortex.

Passengers in both sleighs were knocked out of their seats. The animals pulling the sleighs slammed into each other, becoming tangled and confused.

Green jumped to his feet, searching for the reins, which had been torn from his grasp. He spotted them, dangling from the reindeer harnesses in front of the sleigh.

The sleighs shuddered as they strained against the pull of the Time Expander. The wolves snapped at the reindeer, trying to bite them, their fangs coming close. Tinsel flew lower, dragging his fellow reindeer beneath the reach of the wolves and their threatening jaws.

Green saw the struggle of his reindeer and pulled his Freeze Ray pistol from its holster. He took aim at the hitch connecting the wolves to Cole's sleigh.

Winters saw what Green was doing and, as a result of their years of training together, pieced together Green's plan. Winters quickly looked at Ivy, who was just pulling herself up in Cole's sleigh.

"Green, wait!" shouted Winters.

Green didn't hear Winters in time and fired. A green bolt shot from the Freeze Ray and exploded into the hitch. The wolf pack broke free from Cole's sleigh and were thrown through the distortion into real time.

The wolves tumbled forward and then began to fall. They quickly regrouped and sailed into the night, making their way toward the South Pole.

Back in the vortex, Cole leapt from his sleigh into Santa's as his sleigh dropped out from under him. Cole's sleigh slipped down and hung sideways from the runners of Santa's sleigh.

Santa's reindeer team struggled to keep the two sleighs in the air.

Green looked up ahead and saw that they were on a collision course with a group of skyscrapers. He dove for the reins, but Cole jumped on his back.

Winters raced to the edge of the sleigh to help Ivy. As he looked over the side, he saw Ivy and Frostbite clinging to the seats in Cole's sleigh. They hung down, their feet close to the edge of the distortion of the Time Expander.

"Isaac, I'm slipping!" shouted Ivy.

"Hold on, I'm coming!"

Winters spun around to see Cole on Green's back, his arm tight around Green's throat. Green stretched out his hand, trying to reach the reins dangling from the reindeer.

Cole peered at Winters, his mouth curled in a snarl. "Who you going to save, lover boy? Your new girlfriend or your partner?"

Another jolt rocked the sleighs. Cole's sleigh slipped further off of the runners of Santa's sleigh. If it came clean it would be sucked back into real time at an incredible speed and, without the ability to continue flying, would crash into a building or fall to the ground.

Ivy screamed.

Winters was torn, but stepped forward to help Green, duty winning out. Green put his hand out and spoke through vocal cords clenched in Cole's vice like grip. "No, Isaac, help her!"

Winters nodded and wasted no time, whirling back toward Cole's sleigh. He grabbed a square pack from under the driver's seat and slipped it over his shoulders.

Green and Cole continued to wrestle. "Get . . ." Green grabbed Cole around the neck and flung him over the seat to the back of the sleigh. "Off me!"

Winters jumped over the edge of Santa's sleigh and fell into Cole's, grabbing onto the side railing. Frostbite hoisted himself up and grabbed Winters, who then kicked him in the chest, knocking Frostbite away.

Green reached over the front of the sleigh, struggling to reach the reins. His fingers inched closer and closer. He looked down at Cole's sleigh.

Winters hung by one arm, stretching his hand to Ivy, who hung below him.

"Ivy, grab my hand!"

Ivy tried, but couldn't quite reach.

"I can't!"

Their fingertips were about to touch when Frostbite swung toward Winters and punched him in the chest.

Winters clutched the seat with both hands. Frostbite slunk even closer and grabbed Winters by the jacket.

Green watched their struggle and snagged the reins and pulled, steering the sleighs around a skyscraper just in the nick of time.

The abrupt maneuver rocked the sleighs. Ivy lost her grip and fell, screaming as she disappeared through the distortion, back into real time.

Winters put both of his feet against Frostbite's chest and pushed off, springing through the distortion, sailing after Ivy.

The movement from Winters's dive caused Cole's sleigh to break free from Santa's. Frostbite clung to the seat as the sleigh was pulled through the distortion. "No!" Frostbite screamed, his voice disappearing as he left the vortex.

Freed from the weight of Cole's sleigh, Santa's sleigh flung upward and knocked Green off balance.

Out in real time, Winters and Ivy fell rapidly toward the city below. Winters tucked his arms tight against his sides and willed his body to fall even faster, rocketing to Ivy.

He grabbed Ivy and pulled a cord on the parachute tucked inside his pack. Air hit the chute and shot the two of them upward before they steadied and began to fall slowly toward the ground.

They heard screaming and turned to see Frostbite falling through the air as Cole's sleigh rocketed out of the vortex, sailing past the city.

Frostbite plowed into a giant Garfield balloon, which popped. He grabbed the torn fragments of the balloon and floated to the ground where he was promptly arrested by the NYPD and the SSS. In the distance, Cole's sleigh slammed into the ocean.

Ivy turned and looked into Winters's eyes as they floated gently downward.

"Boy am I glad I met you today," she said.

Winters held Ivy close. She closed her eyes as he kissed her.

Winters grinned, but then remembered Green. His eyes scanned the sky in a panic.

Back inside the vortex, Cole climbed over the seat in Santa's sleigh, panting. Green squared off against him, ready for a fight.

"It's over, Cole. You're finished."

"You must be pretty proud of yourself, Green. Ruining my plans. I'm sure you'll get a nice, shiny medal."

"Your humor is as awful as you are, Cole. Let it go, you're finished."

"I know it's hard to believe, but Santa Claus isn't all he's made out to be, Green Peace. You follow him blindly, but his entire existence is a lie."

Green shook his head; even though he had his own issues with Santa, it upset him to hear others disparage him.

"Santa doesn't even deliver all the presents," said Cole.

"What are you talking about?"

"Like you don't know. You're just as bad as he is, Green. Do you know how many kids you let down every year?"

Green had enough of Cole's stinging words. He lunged at Cole and knocked him to the floor. They wrestled, looking ridiculous as they rolled around, a grown man throttling a tiny elf. Winded, they both stopped for a moment.

"Go stuff a stocking!" yelled Cole.

Green caught his breath. "It takes a real lowlife to try and take out Santa Claus. You've been drinking too much of that rancid milk. It's gone straight to your tiny elf brain."

Cole's eyes burned with anger. He launched himself at Green, jumped on his back, and bit his shoulder.

"Are you biting me?" asked Green, shocked.

Green tried to knock Cole off and slammed him into the Time

131

Expander's control panel, the blow initiating the emergency shut down protocol.

There was a large blast of light all around them and the sleigh throttled as the vortex disassembled. The reindeer broke free from the sleigh.

CHAPTER TWENTY-THREE

B ack in real time, it was night. Rockefeller Square was decorated for the holiday season. A large crowd enjoyed hot chocolate and holiday splendor. Many people were gathered by the famous giant Christmas tree decorated in bright lights. The spectacular tree loomed above the ice skating rink where more people skated, celebrating the beginning of the Christmas season.

A loud sound came from the sky, much like a high-powered generator coming to life. Everyone at Rockefeller Square looked up, surprised by the intense whoosh that seemed to suck air from the night sky. It was followed by a burst of hot white and blue light that ripped through the air.

Santa's sleigh sprung from the effects of the Time Expander, rocketing high above. This distracted the people on the ground from seeing Tinsel and the other reindeer sailing away into the night, heading north.

Santa's sleigh streaked across the skyline before crashing into the gigantic tree at Rockefeller Center. The snow-covered tree acted as a cushion, softening what could have been a lethal blow.

The crowd ran up to the tree to catch a glimpse of the sleigh and the bizarre event they had just witnessed.

High up in the tree, one of the reins from the sleigh was wrapped around Cole's leg as he hung upside down from a branch, his arms and legs dangling. Cole looked down at Green, who was still in the sleigh, wedged between two thick branches on its side.

"Why, Green?" yelled Cole. "Why do you risk your life for Claus? He doesn't care about us."

Green thought for a moment, regaining his wits. "It's my job."

At the sound of commotion below, Green slowly peeked his head out of the sleigh and saw the enormous crowd, which had gathered below. Everyone fell silent.

Green gave an awkward smile and slowly waved. The crowd erupted in thunderous applause, thinking that it all must all be a part of the strange show that had started at the Macy's Thanksgiving Day Parade.

Emergency vehicles rushed onto the scene. Veronica jumped out of a police cruiser and ran toward the tree. Santa and Mrs. Claus followed, surrounded by a handful of SSS Agents and NYPD officers.

The emergency crews removed Green and Cole from the tree. Cole looked to the ice rink. He'd grown up running on ice and now lived in an ice palace. Ice was literally his home and as soon as Cole was free, he streaked onto the rink and skated away, his feet flowing gracefully over the frozen surface. SSS agents and NYPD officers took off after him, slipping and sliding all over the ice.

Liam Parker, an eleven-year-old who had been at the rink with his mother, saw Cole trying to get away from the officials. It had been a long day on the rink and Liam was bored. He was a fantastic skater and had been stifled by the gigantic crowd on the ice, which had made it hard to open up and skate fast. With all of those people now at the edge of the rink, looking up at the tree, the ice was clear except for Cole and the officers.

Liam took off on his skates, gaining steam, flying like a young Bobby Orr across the ice. He got close to Cole and slid on to his side, plowing into the small elf and sending him crashing into a group of SSS agents.

One of the agents helped Liam to his feet. "Nice moves, kid," he said. Liam beamed as the officers slapped handcuffs on to Cole.

As Cole was dragged off the rink, he could see the crowd looking at him, their faces filled with repulsion, disgust, and disappointment. The last thing they were feeling for Cole was adoration. He lowered his head, hiding his face from the flashing cameras and the scornful looks from the crowd.

At the base of the tree, Officer Lyon walked up to Green. "Thank you, Agent Green. We'll take it from here." They shook hands.

Santa waddled toward the group of NYPD officers and SSS agents who were moving Cole toward a police cruiser. Frostbite was already in the back, handcuffed as well.

"Hello, boys. Would you mind giving me some time alone with the elf?" asked Santa.

"Are you sure, sir?" asked one of the agents.

"I'll be fine. It won't take long."

The men left Santa alone with Cole. Cole looked dazed, handcuffed, standing next to the police car.

"Cole," said Santa. He gently put his hand on Cole's shoulder.

Cole looked up, his scowl gone, his eyes cast down, and his head hung low.

"Cole, can you hear me?"

Cole slowly nodded, then looked back down in shame.

"Good, because I want you to hear this. Cole, I forgive you!"

Cole looked back up, his brow scrunched in confusion.

"I forgive you for what you've done. I forgive you for what you've tried to do," said Santa.

Cole stood silent, all emotion gone from his face.

"I know that deep inside of you is a good elf. You'll have to pay for what you've done, but I'll put in a good word for you, and just between you and me, my word carries a lot of weight, ho, ho." Santa laughed at his pun, but got serious again. "And I just want you to know, if you ever want to come back, you'll be welcome at the North Pole! I mean it."

Cole couldn't look at Santa, deep with shame.

"Very well," said Santa before he turned to walk away.

Cole looked up. "Santa?" his voice shook.

Santa turned around. "Yes, Cole?"

"Why? Why do you forgive me? I must be the naughtiest, worst elf of all time."

Santa smiled. "That's not what I see."

Cole knew the words he needed to say, but it had been years since he'd even thought them. He steadied himself and looked Santa straight in the eye. "Thank you."

Santa winked at Cole, then nodded his head and walked away.

An NYPD officer opened the rear door and ushered Cole inside.

Green and Veronica stood side-by-side, leaning on each other, exhausted and overwhelmed by the chaotic aftermath of Cole's plan.

"Covering all of this up is going to be a giant PR nightmare," said Veronica. "So many people witnessed all of this."

"I think you're going to be surprised by how few people actually saw anything," said Green.

Veronica was confused.

"I got this." Green walked a few yards to where crowd control barriers had been placed and large groups of people stood gawking. TV reporters and cameramen were there as well.

Green waved to gather the crowd's attention.

"Ladies and gentlemen, let me have your attention! I have an important update! There was an assassination attempt on Santa Claus by one of his former elves. Fortunately he was saved by his secret service and the Abominable Snowman. There was a huge sleigh chase over the city. Luckily we were able to freeze time and space by accelerating faster than the speed of light and save Santa's life. The chase ended when Santa's sleigh crashed into that tree."

The crowd grumbled.

"That's real funny, smart guy," said a man in the crowd.

"I don't understand this kind of street theater," said a woman, shaking her head.

"I bet this all has something to do with Justin Timberlake!" exclaimed a teenage girl. Others cheered at the prospect.

The crowd began to disperse just as fast as it formed, getting back to enjoying the tree, the ice rink, and the beginning of the Christmas season.

Green walked back to Veronica.

"See? People refuse to believe the truth, even when it's right in front of them."

"I've noticed that about some people," said Veronica, giving Green a slight, warm smile.

"Touché, Miss Snow."

Veronica wrapped her arm around Green's. "Noel?" Veronica took her other hand and turned his face to her.

Green felt all the stress and angst of the day fade away as he saw her looking up at him. "Yes?"

She looked lovingly into his eyes. "Was there ever a time in your life when you believed in Santa Claus?"

Green was about to answer glibly, but something stopped him. He saw the sincerity in her face, felt the tenderness in her voice. He took his time and answered slowly, "Yes."

Veronica smiled. "That's the person I need you to be from now on." She pulled Green close, hugging him.

Green hugged her back; he felt something deep inside begin to raise to the surface. It was something that he hadn't felt in a long time. He knew there was a word for it, but he couldn't quite place it. Then, as Veronica pulled back and looked at him again, he found the word. *Home.*

A horse-drawn carriage approached Rockefeller Center. Ivy and Winters sat close together in the back. She was snuggled up against him and he had an arm around her shoulders. The driver stopped the carriage in the middle of the crowd.

Green and Veronica held hands and approached the carriage.

"Well, well, you're alive after all," said Green. "I thought I'd never see you again."

"You should be so lucky," replied Winters as he helped Ivy exit the carriage.

"Ivy, this is Veronica Snow and Agent Noel Green."

Ivy shook hands with Veronica and Green.

"Nice to meet you, Ivy," said Green. "Impressive how much I've heard about you in one day."

Ivy blushed. Winters hugged her close to him.

"I'm exhausted," said Green. "Let's go home."

As the small group turned to go, a very serious-looking man, about forty, Inspector Spenser, approached Green from behind. Spenser wore a suit and had an official United Nations identification hanging from his suit jacket.

"Agent Green?"

Green turned around to see Spenser.

"My name is Inspector Spenser, with a special unit of the UN. May I have a word with you?"

Green turned to the others in his group. "Give me a minute."

The others continued on to the cars as Green gave Spenser his full attention.

"How can I help you, Inspector Spenser?"

Spenser handed Green a large manila case folder. Green quickly thumbed through the file, stopping on a sheet of paper containing a hand-painted graphic of a white elephant.

"What is this?" asked Green.

"Have you ever heard of *White Elephant*, Agent Green?"

"No, what is it?"

"We aren't entirely sure, but we've been picking up quite a bit of chatter about them and some of the evidence suggests that Mr. Claus and the North Pole may be at risk."

"Well, we will keep a sharp eye out," said Green.

"See that you do. Something tells me this group is up to no good."

"That's our job, Inspector. Thank you for bringing this to my attention."

Spenser gave Green his card. Green shook hands with Spenser before turning and joining back up with the group.

"What was that?" asked Winters.

Green handed him the file. "Another potential threat."

"White Elephant?" Winters read the file.

Veronica sidled up to Green. "Is everything okay?"

Green took her hand in his. "Never better."

CHAPTER TWENTY-FOUR

Hundreds of SSS agents sat at their terminals in the control center at the North Pole. It was Christmas Eve and they had experienced another successful night. There were only a few deliveries left.

Agent Burke worked at her desk. She spoke over her headset. "Sugarplum Fairy, be advised the street history for Oakwood Lane shows a Class One Naughty, Stephanie Amber Kelly, ten years old. Over."

The pilot's voice came back over Burke's headset. "Roger that, Nutcracker, initiating ground operations now. Over."

Burke turned as Green entered the room. He looked the same as the year before. "Everyone, listen up," said Green. "You've all done a fantastic job this year and I anticipate that the rest of the night will play out successfully. I want to thank each and every one of you for your exceptional service and dedication to the job at hand here. The big guy couldn't do what he does without every single one of you. We have a slight change this year, per Mr. Claus's orders; every single SSS agent will have time off on Christmas."

There was a hum of excitement and appreciation in the room. The agents all stood and gave a standing ovation. Green cracked a brief smile.

Green entered the Northern Lights Tavern. It was packed full of North Pole employees, elves, leprechauns, and people, all celebrating another successful year.

Green made his way through the crowd to a table where his friends were waiting for him: Winters, Ivy, and Veronica. The ladies wore beautiful Christmas dresses; Ivy's was red with white lace while Veronica's was more symbolic. Her dress was *green*.

"There you are, Green," said Winters. "We thought you were a no show. I've been sitting here with these two gorgeous ladies all to myself."

"I'm sorry, I got held up in Ops."

Green sat down next to Veronica, giving her a quick kiss.

"The McKenzie twins?" asked Winters.

"And a few newcomers. Every year, without fail."

Avalanche crept up behind Green and put his mammoth hands over his Green's eyes. "GESSS HHHUUUUGH!"

"Hmmm, let me see. Massive hairy hands, a very distinctive speech pattern. Hmmm. Is it Avalanche?"

"MEEEEE!"

Green stood and let Avalanche hug him. "Hello, buddy. Merry Christmas."

"He's been riding the mechanical bull all night," said Veronica. "He loves it."

"Didn't he get shot in New York?" asked Green.

"Yes, but don't you know that abominable snowmen heal ten times faster than humans?" Veronica smiled at Green.

"A handy attribute," said Green.

A waitress brought out a couple of buckets of eggnog for Avalanche. A few leprechauns came running up to Avalanche.

"Come on, boy'o! Let's go ride that mechanical beast again," said one of the leprechauns.

Avalanche put one of the leprechauns on his shoulders and headed in the direction of the mechanical bull.

Winters poured everyone a glass of eggnog. "I would like to propose a toast."

The other three picked up their drinks.

"To love and friendship, the very best gifts of all."

They all put their glasses in for cheers.

CHAPTER TWENTY-FIVE

Green walked in through the front door of his cottage. He'd had a nice time with Veronica, Winters, and Ivy, but he was exhausted. He was looking forward to a long winter's nap.

A silhouette stood in his living room. Green quickly turned on the lights and found Santa beaming at him.

"Sir?"

"Sorry, Noel. I didn't mean to scare you."

"Not at all, sir. You're welcome any time."

Santa walked over closer to Green. "I have almost finished another year of successful gift delivery. This is the last house on my route, the most important stop of all."

Green shifted. "I don't understand."

Santa took out a small, dusty, faded wrapped gift. "This is for you, Noel! Merry Christmas, my friend."

Santa handed Green the box. Green noticed a tag that said *undeliverable.*

"Um, thank you, sir. I, uh, I didn't get you anything. I didn't realize we were exchanging gifts . . ."

"No, no, this has been a long time coming. I don't usually do this, but would you mind if I watched you open it?"

Green shrugged his shoulders. "No, that would be fine."

He slowly unwrapped the gift and took the top off of a small box. A thin silver box lay within that said *Secret Spy Series.* Green was speechless. He slid back the lid and took out a space age silver watch, the watch of his boyhood dreams.

"I don't understand," said Green.

"I hear it even talks and that you can go under water with it!"

Green smiled and shifted uncomfortably, not sure how to react.

"I'm sorry it's late, Noel Green from 3214 Cicero Street, Apartment 2D, Chicago, Illinois," said Santa, smiling.

"Thank you, sir. I've always wanted one of these."

"I know you have."

"Did I do something wrong when I was younger? Is that why you didn't come?"

"You didn't do anything wrong, son, far from it. You were one of my very best; top of the nice list, year after year, in fact."

"Then why, sir? Why didn't you ever visit my house?"

"I've been doing this a very, very long time, Noel. If it were up to me, every girl and boy would get the gift they ask for at Christmas. But it's not. We've got a whole warehouse full of these *undeliverable* packages. With some children, there are circumstances that are out of my control. In some cases, there are homes where I'm not welcome."

Green nodded. "My father."

"Your father was a good man, Noel, but grown-ups sometimes lose faith and blame their misfortunes on those who could help them."

143

"And all these years I thought . . ."

"HO, HO, HO! Noel, today you're one of the most important people in the North Pole. You're the one that I trust with my very own life. I hope it's not too late for you to believe in me." Santa put his hand on Green's shoulder. "Because I sure believe in you."

Green was overcome with emotion, deeply moved by Santa's gesture. "It's never too late . . ." He smiled up at Santa, realizing that he'd echoed one of Santa's long-held sentiments. "Thank you, sir."

"Thank you, Noel. Merry Christmas."

"Merry Christmas," said Green as he put the watch on around his wrist, checking it out in the light; he looked like a kid . . . on Christmas.

Santa smiled. "Now, if you don't mind, I've been going up and down chimneys all night. I wonder if I could just go out your front door?"

"Go right ahead, sir."

"Excellent! It's so much easier. I don't even know why I started going down chimneys in the first place. We do weird things when we're young! Ho, ho, ho!"

Santa left by the front door. Green stood in his living room and stared at his watch.

Veronica was asleep in her giant, cozy bed. Her phone rang.

She threw her arm out of the bed and felt around for the phone. "Hello?"

Green's voice shouted back: "Merry Christmas! Rise and shine!"

"What? Noel, is that you? What time is it?"

"Now, don't tell me you're still in bed on a beautiful Christmas morning like this?"

Veronica looked at her windows. "It's dark outside."

"It's the North Pole; it's always dark outside. I'm coming over right now, and I'll be there quick, so you'd better not still be in bed when I get there."

"What? Now?" She hung up the phone, sat up, and looked at her clock. "Five in the morning, are you kidding me, Green?" She stumbled out of bed in her pajamas.

She heard a noise coming from the front of her cottage. Slowly, she made her way into the living room.

Hitting a light switch, she found Green standing in the middle of the room, surrounded by hundreds of white roses. She raised her eyebrows in surprise.

"When I said I'd get here quick, I really meant it."

Veronica looked over the flowers. She brought a hand to her mouth and fought back her emotions. "They're beautiful."

"Three hundred and sixty-six snow-white roses. One for each day that I've known and loved you," said Green.

"Noel, that's the sweetest thing . . ."

"I *do* love you, Miss Veronica Snow. I've loved you since the very first time I laid eyes on you. It just took me a while to believe it."

Veronica smiled and looked into Green's eyes. She grabbed Green's hand and pulled him to the other side of the room. She lined him up under the mistletoe hanging from her ceiling.

"I didn't think I would actually get to use this," she said.

Green pulled her close to him and put his arms around her. She reached up and put her arms around his neck. They shared a beautiful romantic kiss, worth waiting a year for.

"I love you too, Agent Noel Green."

"Merry Christmas, Miss Snow."

They kissed again.

Green pulled back, looking Veronica in the eyes. "I want to take you for a ride in Santa's sleigh."

Veronica laughed. "A year ago I would have said you're crazy."

"And now?"

It was still Christmas morning, still dark outside. Green was flying Santa's sleigh with Tinsel and the B-team.

Veronica cuddled next to Green, her head on his shoulder. They were both bundled up in warm clothing. A thick red blanket with white trimming covered their laps.

They flew through the spectacular Northern Lights. Beautiful bright colors surrounded the sleigh, dancing and swirling as they sailed. Veronica couldn't imagine a more romantic view. She grabbed Green's hand. He looked over at her and smiled.

"This year, for the first time in my life, I got everything I wanted for Christmas," said Green.

Veronica gave him a small kiss.

The sleigh flew off into the colored sky, passing more than a few clouds. The temperature dropped, and soon dust and other particles would enter the clouds and the cold would cause water vapor to freeze to them. Flakes would form, gain mass, and begin their descent to the earth below. It would snow again, bringing with it a pristine whiteness and the promise of another Christmas.

EPILOGUE

Former SSS agent Arnold Black trudged through a seemingly endless field of white snow. He'd been walking for days, fueled with hatred and disappointment at being left behind by Cole. He'd seen that Cole's plan had failed and that he'd been arrested. The news had been silent on just where he was being held or if there would be any trial. It was out of Black's control now.

Black had no place to go. He'd betrayed the SSS, Santa, and the North Pole, and his new home at the South Pole had been destroyed.

Black felt he had only *one* choice left, only one he could turn to. He'd made his way up north as a stowaway on a cruise ship filled with people celebrating the holidays. That's where he'd been able to see the news and find out that this year's Christmas had been a success and that presents had indeed been delivered.

He'd stolen some winter gear from a cabin on board and he now looked like an explorer with the thick fur-lined coat, goggles, and all.

He trudged to a location south of the North Pole, near the Forbidden Lands of Black Ice. He'd never been out this far and knew that there was a reason the word *forbidden* was in the area's name. He'd heard all of the tales of Santa Claus and Pole One and the great war, but had thought they were just stories the elves had made up to inflate their own importance. However, when working with Cole he'd found a journal written by Cole's father. Black now believed many of the stories to be true and that the one he now sought wasn't a figment of elfin imagination, but was a true and living being.

Legend had it that oil flowed under the fields of white ice and that at certain points you could see rivers of fire beneath the ice.

Black now knew that the legend was true. He had seen pockets of fire deep beneath the ice.

Black walked over an area where burning oil had broken free from the ice, forming black stalagmites, some of the only ones in the world *outside* a cave. It was hard trudging across the terrain, but Black had finally found what he was looking for, and he pressed forward.

In the distance he could see the infamous Black Ice Tower, home to the one he sought. As Black moved closer, a large man moved from behind one of the outgrowths in the ice. The man had the appearance of a beast with thick hair and claws, but Black could see that it was a man wearing a fur coat and animal skins draped over his body and gloves with ice picks on the ends of the fingers.

The man held up a single ice-picked finger, halting Black in his tracks. "Are you lost?" asked the man.

"I don't think so," said Black.

"Who are you?"

"Who are *you*?"

"I am Rufus," said the man. "And nobody gets past this point unless I say so."

"My name is Arnold Black and I am an ex-agent of the SSS."

Rufus pulled a staff from behind his back. The tip of the staff glowed with a blue light.

Black put up his hands. "I said ex, as in I *left* the SSS and betrayed Claus! I am now his enemy!"

Rufus lowered his staff. "You're former SSS?"

"Yes. And I have information your boss will want to hear. I know who you work for and I want to see him. I want to see him right now."

Rufus shook his head. "Do you really? What's his name?"

Black smiled. "Krampus."

The name hung in the air between Black and Rufus. It was a name rarely spoken and it had a powerful impact.

Rufus stared at Black. He hadn't expected him to know. He thought it over. "Come with me," he said.

Rufus led Black around another outcropping to a cluster of black rock formed by burning oil over thousands of years. They entered a cave-like chamber; the walls were black rock, the floor was clear ice.

Rufus grabbed a torch from a holder on the wall and allowed Black to follow him inside the black rock chamber.

As Black entered, the glow from the torch flickered, casting shadows on the walls. He saw something scrawled on the wall. He peered closer to get a better look.

It was a hand-painted white elephant.

THE END

ABOUT THE AUTHORS

Richard Grant Bennett worked in the art department on *The Terminal, Charlie and the Chocolate Factory*, and *Corpse Bride*. He is a writer and designer for *The AquaBats! Super Show!* and was an executive producer on *Ben Banks*. Richard and his wife Amber live in the Salt Lake area with their two children.

Bryce Clark is the author of the children's book *Red Shirt Kids*. He wrote and directed the independent film *Beauty and the Least: The Misadventures of Ben Banks*, starring Mischa Barton, and has written for the TV show *Yo Gabba Gabba!* Bryce wrote and will direct the upcoming film *Phobic*. Bryce and his wife Stephanie live in the Salt Lake area with their five children.

Jason deVilliers is the cocreator of *The Aquabats! Super Show!* He produced the film *The Flyboys*, starring Tom Sizemore and Stephen Baldwin. Jason directed, wrote, and edited multiple episodes of *Yo Gabba Gabba!* and edited and executive produced *Ben Banks*. Jason and his wife Kelly live in Southern California with their two children.